HIGH PRAISE FOR ROBERT J. RANDISI!

"Randisi always turns out a traditional Western with plenty of gunplay and interesting characters."

—*Roundup*

"Each of Randisi's novels is better than its entertaining predecessor."

—*Booklist*

"Everybody seems to be looking for the next Louis L'Amour. To me, they need look no further than Randisi."

—Jake Foster, Author of *Three Rode South*

"Randisi knows his stuff and brings it to life."

—*Preview Magazine*

"Randisi has a definite ability to construct a believable plot around his characters."

—*Booklist*

LUCKY SHOT

"Señor, I am sure you have taken the wrong attitude. We are not bandidos, we are just a little bit down on our luck. We would appreciate it if you could help us out."

"No."

Gold Tooth's face went from amiable to stern.

"Señor, please, you are being insulting."

"Not yet," Decker said, "but I'll be getting there soon if you and your friend don't ride...now!"

"Ay-yay-yay-yay," Gold Tooth said, shaking his head at the gringo's folly.

His compadre was obviously watching Gold Tooth closely, for when the leader made his move for his gun, so did the other man.

Decker never even pulled his sawed-off, cut-down shotgun from its holster. He simply swiveled his holster up and fired that way. The cloud of double-o came out and spread just enough to catch both men. Had they remained side by side he might have missed one, but in moving back the second man had positioned himself not perfectly, but certainly more helpfully, giving the shot pattern time to spread. At the proper distance, a shotgun is simply a devastating weapon that not only kills, but disfigures and dismembers as well.

ROBERT J. RANDISI

The Lawman

LEISURE BOOKS NEW YORK CITY

PWES
Randisi

To Gordon Shirreffs.

A LEISURE BOOK®

December 2008

Published by

Dorchester Publishing Co., Inc.
200 Madison Avenue
New York, NY 10016

ISBN 10: 0-8439-6126-0
ISBN 13: 978-0-8439-6126-3

Visit us on the web at www.dorchesterpub.com.

The Lawman

Prologue I

Pemberton, Colorado Territory

Johnny "Red" Moran woke to a warm presence next to him. A warm, naked presence.

He frowned, trying to remember who it was without looking. Finally, he had to give up, turn over and take a look.

Hell, that didn't help. She was naked and blonde, but he couldn't remember her name.

"Wake up!" he said, slapping her on the ass.

"Hey!"

The girl's head snapped up and she looked around. Red got a good look at her face then, but the name still didn't come to him.

"Good morning, honey," she said, smiling.

She shouldn't have smiled. She had a decent body, though a little heavy in the breasts and flanks, but her teeth were bad. She really shouldn't have smiled.

"Time for you to get moving," he said.

"Now?" she asked. "It's early."

"It's gettin' later all the time."

She frowned at him, then said, "You don't remember my name, do you?"

"No, I don't. Get out."

She sat up so he could see her breasts. They were large and beginning to sag. From behind she looked like a girl, but from the front he could see that she was creeping up on thirty pretty quick.

"You ready to give me a waker-upper?"

"I'm always ready, honey."

He slid his hand down over her fleshy belly to her thigh, where he pinched her flesh between his fingers.

"Oh—" she said, closing her eyes and biting her bottom lip in pain. "Hey—"

"I told you to get out," he said, "and I meant it." He let her go and snapped, "Now get dressed and get out."

"Okay, okay," she said, her eyes wet with pain.

She stood up and he watched her as she hurriedly dressed. If she was the best this town had to offer him after two months, then it was time to move on.

When she was dressed she rushed to the door and opened it, then stopped and turned.

"Mandy," she said.

"What?"

"My name is Mandy," she said, and then burst into tears and ran from the room.

"Jesus," he said, shaking his head.

Moran got dressed, strapped on his gun, chucked some belongings into his saddlebags and carried them downstairs with him.

"Goin' someplace, Sheriff?" the desk clerk asked.

"No place in particular, Jed."

He left the hotel and walked over to the livery stable.

"Would you mind saddling my horse, Arnold?" he asked the towheaded sixteen-year-old who worked there.

"Sure, Sheriff. Goin' someplace?"

"No place special, son."

When his horse was saddled, Red Moran, sheriff of Pemberton, rode him over to the bank. He sat tall in the saddle, tall and wide shouldered. No one knew why Moran called himself "Red." It certainly wasn't because he had red hair. He had hair so blond that it sometimes seemed as if he had no hair at all. Still, when asked what people should call him, he always answered, "Call me Red."

And so they did.

Sheriff Red Moran.

Moran had been sheriff of six different towns in the last eight months, towns that had been looking for lawmen. When he got tired of a town he moved on, and he usually got tired within two or three months.

Before he moved on, though, there was something he had to do—something he always did.

He went to the bank.

He left his horse outside and walked into the bank. It was early, and there were only two customers. He asked the teller to get the bank manager, Mr. Hampton.

"Sure, Sheriff."

When Hampton came out he said, "What can I do for you, Sheriff?"

"I'm taking a trip, Mr. Hampton, and I need to make a withdrawal."

Orville Hampton frowned.

"I wasn't aware that you had an account with the bank, Sheriff," the older man said. He was in his late fifties, at least fifteen years older than Moran, a stocky man who wore three-piece suits.

"I don't," Moran said, "but I'm making a withdrawal anyway."

"You mean you want a loan?" Hampton said in an effort to understand what the sheriff was driving at.

"No, I mean I'm making a withdrawal."

"I don't understand," Hampton said, confused. "How much—"

"Just take a sack and fill it up, Mr. Hampton," Moran said. He drew his gun, pointed it at the bank manager and added, "Now."

"W–what—what are you doing?"

"I just told you. I'm making a withdrawal."

"B–but you can't. You're the sheriff!"

"Not anymore. I got bored, and I need some travelling money."

"This town has treated you good, man! How can you do this?"

"This makes it easy," Moran said, waving his gun. "Now tell your teller here to fill up a sack. The rest of you just stand easy."

The customers, a middle-aged woman and an older man, watched in shock as their sheriff robbed the bank.

"I won't," Hampton said.

"Mr. Hampton—" the teller said.

"This is outrageous!"

"Mr. Hampton—"

"Don't make this hard, Mr. Hampton. It's a simple transaction."

"I won't do it!" Hampton said firmly.

Moran took two steps forward and smacked the barrel of his pistol against the bank manager's head. Hampton slumped to the floor, barely breathing.

"What about you, sonny?" Moran asked the teller.

"I'm filling a sack, Sheriff, I'm filling a sack."

"Good boy."

When the canvas sack was filled the teller handed it to Moran, who backed towards the door.

"I'd advise you people to stay inside for a while after I leave."

He went out the door, mounted his horse and rode out.

Heading for the next town that badly needed a sheriff.

The people in the bank were all thinking the same thing. Their bank had been robbed, the bank manager pistol-whipped, and what they would normally do in that instance would be to send for the sheriff, who would then get up a posse.

Only their sheriff had just robbed their bank. Once, Red Moran had been an honest sheriff in a Wyoming town, but eventually he had gotten tired of having the townspeople look down on him. For the most part they considered him their elected servant, and they treated him as such. He got a free meal here and a free drink there, and when things went right everybody was happy, but let just one thing go wrong, and they were ready to kick him out of office.

Well, one day he just up and kicked himself out of office. He had gone over to the bank, robbed it, rode out and never looked back.

Five more times he had done that, finding five towns who needed a sheriff very badly. Moran's biggest weapon was his innocent face, and he used it to his best advantage.

He still had all six badges that he'd worn, for he always kept the badge as a souvenir.

Now he'd take the money from the Pemberton bank, ride on down to Mexico, piss it away on food and booze and whores, and then come back over the border and find himself another town.

It was as easy as that.

Prologue II

Hastings, Kansas

Decker paused in front of the Hastings, Kansas, sheriff's office to read the posters that were affixed to the oustide wall. There were a few possibilities, but the one that caught his eye was a poster for a man named Moran.

The poster also called him "The Lawman."

It explained that Moran had ridden into six different towns, gotten himself appointed sheriff and then within anywhere from two weeks to two months he would up and rob the bank and leave town. The latest case in point was a town called Pemberton, in the Colorado Territory, and that had been a scant week ago. The poster was very recent.

The drawing on the poster showed a man with a face that was easy to trust. It was smooth and youthful, even though the poster gave his age as thirty-five.

This one would be interesting, he thought. He pulled the poster down off the wall and studied it.

What irony, he thought, a bounty hunter tracking down "The Lawman."

"Does that one suit your fancy, bounty hunter?" a voice asked.

Decker looked up and saw the sheriff of Hastings, Kevin Randle, a man he knew well enough to call by his first name—which by no means meant that they were friends.

"This fella is sure giving you and yours a bad name, Kevin."

"Go after him, then." Randle reached over and tapped the poster with his forefinger. "This is one time I wouldn't mind seeing you make some money."

As the sheriff went into his office Decker looked at the poster again. The reward was twenty-five hundred dollars, because in Pemberton "The Lawman" had made one big mistake.

He had hit the bank manager too hard, and the man had died.

So added to the bank robbery charges in six territories was the charge of murder in one.

Decker took the poster with him and went into the sheriff's office.

"That the one you're takin'?" the sheriff asked from behind his desk. He had poured himself a cup of coffee, but he did not offer Decker one.

"This looks like the one. How much do you know about him, Kevin?"

Randle shrugged. He was a youngish man—early thirties or so—and had worn a badge in this town for about three years. Before that he'd been a deputy in several other places.

"Just what every other lawman in the country knows. He hits a town and then lays low for a while before hitting another one. Rides in, becomes sheriff, stays anywhere from two weeks to two months, then robs the bank and rides out again. Boom, disappears for weeks, months at a time."

"Spending the money."

"Most likely. He sure as hell don't seem to be saving it."

"That kind never does. What about the badges?" Randle frowned.

"What about 'em?"

"Does he leave them behind?"

"Damned if I know that. Why?"

"Just wanted to know all the facts before I took out after him."

"I do know one thing about him."

"What?"

"He's a pretty arrogant sonofabitch!"

"Why do you say that?"

"He uses his real name. He used to be a lawman, you know, a legitimate lawman in Wyoming. He robbed the town he worked in for two years, and he's been going ever since. Six towns in thirteen months."

"Where's he been concentrating?"

"All over, never the same state or the same territory twice. The Wyoming Territory, the Dakotas, Nebraska, Nevada, the Utah Territory, and the Colorado Territory. Also, you'd think that using his real name he'd have built up a reputation that would warn people." Randle shook his head. "The only people who know him are lawmen and bounty hunters, because we read the posters. Why, I'll bet that the people in the towns he's robbed think they're the only ones he hit."

"Well, maybe his own arrogance will trip him up."

"Well, as much as I don't like bounty hunters, Decker, this is one bounty I'd like to see you collect. This yahoo is wanted dead or alive, and it don't make no never mind to me or any decent lawman how you bring him back."

Randle was dead serious.

"That's nice to know, Kevin. Thanks for the information."

Yep, this one should be *real* interesting.

Chapter One

Pemberton wasn't a big town, but as small towns go it appeared to have pretty much everything a town should have.

Decker noticed this as he rode down Pemberton's main street.

They had a livery, a hardware store, a hotel, a saloon, a haberdasher's shop, a gunsmith's shop, one of everything a town needed to survive and prosper.

The only thingh they didn't have anymore was a sheriff—unless, of course, they had elected one during the two weeks since "The Lawman" had robbed their bank.

Decker put his horse up in the livery and went over to the saloon for a drink.

"Help ya?" the bartender asked.

It was after noon, and the saloon was doing a brisk business. It was the only saloon in town, so anyone who wanted a drink would have to go there.

"Beer, cold."

"As cold as we can get it."

Which turned out not to be cold enough, but Decker didn't complain. At least it was wet, and it cut through the dust.

"Got a sheriff in this town?" Decker asked.

"That's sort of a sore point right now, Mister."

"Oh? Why's that?"

"We had a sheriff, but two weeks ago he upped and robbed the bank and left town."

"You don't say?"

"Ain't been able to get anybody to take the job regular since then. Fact is, we had the same problem just afore our last sheriff came into town."

"You made a stranger the sheriff?"

The man shrugged his beefy shoulders.

"He said he wanted the job, and nobody else did, so the mayor and the town council hired him."

"No election?"

"Wasn't nobody wanted to run against him."

"You mean you can't find anybody in this whole town who wants to be sheriff?"

"Town's mostly made up of merchants, Mister. Ain't a lawman among 'em." The man leaned forward then and said, "Say, you wouldn't be looking for a job, would you?"

"After what happened you'd still be willing to hire a stranger?"

"A town needs a sheriff, don't it?"

"Sometimes I wonder," Decker said. He paid for the beer and asked where he could find the mayor.

"His office is down the street, above the general store."

"Thanks."

"Gonna apply for the job?"

Decker ignored the question and left the saloon.

He stopped at the bank first and found the teller who'd been on duty when the bank was robbed.

"It was terrible," the boy said. "It was like Mr. Hampton—that was the manager's name—like he didn't believe the sheriff was serious."

"You did, though?"

"Mister, if a man is pointin' a gun at me, I'm gonna figure he's serious."

"Smart lad."

Decker started to leave, then remembered a question he wanted to ask and turned back.

"How much did he get?"

"About twenty thousand."

Decker whistled softly. A man could lay low a long time with that kind of money.

Next, Decker went over to talk to the mayor. An officious, blustering fool, the mayor had little to tell him about the sheriff.

"He was a total stranger when we hired him, and a total stranger when he left."

"He didn't make any friends while he was here?"

"None. He kept to himself."

"No women?"

"A lot of women, but no one in particular."

"Did he do his job?"

"Well enough—until he robbed us. I tell you, it's a disgrace what that man did, betraying the trust the people of this town put in him."

"Next time you'll know better than to hire a stranger without some sort of references."

Decker left the office, disgusted with the man and the town, thinking that people who won't help themselves deserve whatever they get.

Decker had dinner in a small café and then went to the saloon for a beer. He took a back table and watched the townsmen at play.

It was his routine to spend a day in the last town that his prey had been seen in, collecting any background information that was available. Before taking out after a man, he tried to form a picture of him beyond a physical description or drawing.

Moran was an ex-lawman, and apparently had been a competent one. He was able to get people to trust him and hire him, which meant that he could relate to people when he wanted to. He was arrogant, but he could control his arrogance when he needed to. He didn't bother trying to get on with people once he had the job, and he stayed to himself.

Since the mayor indicated that there had been many women, it seemed he was attractive to them, unless he dealt solely with whores.

So far, Decker had seen one of everything in Pemberton. That meant it had to have a whore-house.

He went to the bar and asked the bartender, who verified his guess. He obtained directions, and went over there.

*   *   *

The madam was a Milly Smith—Miss Milly—a woman in her mid-fifties who must have been a beauty when she was younger. She still had dark hair and an impressive bosom, but everything else had thickened on her and she was fighting a losing battle against aging with corsets, girdles and makeup.

"Sheriff Moran? Sure, he came in here from time to time, but he sure didn't need to."

"Why's that?"

"Women threw themselves at him."

"He was handsome, then?"

"Not 'specially. He had an innocent, wide-eyed look that drew women to him, though. Of course, after spending a night—or even an hour—with him, they found out he wasn't so wide-eyed or innocent."

"Did he mistreat them?"

"He beat up a couple of my girls and I had to talk to him."

"Did you tell the mayor, or the town council?"

"Are you kidding? We finally got a sheriff in this town, they would have figured a few bruises on my girls was a price worth paying."

"You didn't figure it that way, though?"

"Hell, no. I told him that if he put one more bruise on any of my girls I'd ban him from the place. Hell, my stock ain't that great to begin with. I can't afford having them looked knocked around. He behaved after that."

"But he had some women outside of here?"

"I'm sure, though I couldn't name any."

"Couldn't, or wouldn't?"

"Same thing."

"That means he wasn't above having a married woman from time to time."

"You said that, I didn't."

"All right, Miss Milly, thanks for your time."

"Sure you don't want to spend some time upstairs with one of the girls?"

"Nope. I'll be leaving in the morning and I've got to get my rest."

"Pity, they would have liked you—but I don't blame you. I ain't got a one that's worth spit."

"Like you were in your day?"

"Hell, I could put these girls to shame now, if I wanted to, but my days of whorin' are over. Still, if a man took a shine to me there wouldn't have to be any money changing hands."

Decker decided that if that was an invitation he was going to play dumb and pretend he didn't read it right.

"Well, thanks again, Miss Milly."

"Sure," she sighed. "Glad to help."

When Decker left the whorehouse he thought about returning to the saloon, but he knew if he did that he'd end up in a poker game. If he did that, it would end up being a late night, and he wanted to get an early start in the morning.

He went back to his room and stretched out on the bed, fully clothed. He hung his gunbelt on the bedpost, within easy reach.

He had a picture of Red Moran now—a lawman gone bad. And yet, until this town, he had never killed anyone. That meant that killing the bank manager had been an accident. Moran probably didn't even realize that he'd killed a man. Faced with that when the time came, maybe Moran would give himself up. Maybe there was enough real lawman left in him for that.

The question now was, where did Moran go after robbing the bank? Where had he gone all the other times? To the same place?

So far, his jobs had been concentrated around the midwest. He had pulled none heading south, in Texas or New Mexico or Arizona.

Decker made his decision.

Come morning he was heading for Mexico.

Where else would a man hole up with money to spend?

Chapter Two

Decker had been to Mexico on many occasions, and he took the same route each time. He knew which small towns to stop in for a meal and a bed, where the waterholes were when a town wasn't nearby and what homesteads willingly offered meals to travellers.

What you never knew about Mexico from trip to trip was who was in power, and who was fighting to get them out of power.

Actually, Decker didn't care who was in power, just as he didn't particularly care who was the present President of the United States. He didn't care for politics at all, and ignored it unless it was totally impossible.

Decker wanted to live his life his way, at his pace, and to hell with everything else.

Of course, living his life his way meant hunting down men who had broken laws—laws sent up by politicians—but he chose to ignore this tenuous political connection between politicians and his chosen profession.

Bandidos were always a problem in Mexico, but

again Decker had made enough trips to that side of the border that many of the bandit bands knew enough to leave him be.

He liked Mexico, and often thought that if he ever had enough money, he'd settle there.

Decker had bank accounts in banks in different parts of the country. He probably could have retired now if he wanted to, but he was too young to retire. He wasn't thirty-five yet, and what would a man that young do if he retired?

And who was to say when you had enough money?

How much is ever enough?

It was just getting dark when Decker topped a rise and looked down at the adobe ranch house. It was fairly large, and he knew that inside there were four rooms. Though there was no stock in the corral next to it, the corral itself was in good shape, which indicated that perhaps someone still lived there.

Tomàs.

He rode down towards the house, and before he reached it the front door opened and a man stepped out.

It was Tomàs de la Vega, holding a rifle.

"Tomàs," Decker said, "it's been a year, but have I changed that much?"

Vega frowned, stared and then his face relaxed and he lowered his rifle.

But he did not smile.

"Decker."

"You remember."

"Of course. Step down."

Decker dismounted.

"How long do you intend to stay?" Tomàs asked.

"A hot meal and a night's sleep is what I am after, Tomàs."

"You have it, then. Tend to your horse, and I will tend to dinner."

Decker took his horse over to the corral, wondering why Tomàs and not his wife, Estralita, was cooking dinner.

He found out soon enough.

When he entered the house dinner was already on the table. Tortillas, rice and beans, bread, a pot of coffee and a bottle of tequila.

Decker looked around and saw that the house had fallen into a sad state. There were clothes everywhere, torn curtains on the window, and dust, layers of dust, which Estralita would never allow, unless . . .

"Estralita died eight months ago, amigo," Tomàs said, sitting opposite Decker.

Looking closely at Tomàs now, Decker could see that the man was in as bad shape—or worse—than the house. There were dark circles under his eyes, he hadn't shaved, his eyes were bloodshot, his shirt dirty and he looked sixty rather than forty.

"I'm sorry, Tomàs. How did she die?"

"Three men came while I was away on business. They raped her and killed her."

That jolted Decker. Estralita had not been a beautiful woman, but she had been vital and energetic, and it made you feel alive just to watch her move. She had not only died, she had been violated and murdered.

"Tomàs—"

"I hunted them," Tomàs said with no emotion in his voice. "I found two of them, one after the other, and I tortured them, and killed them. I never found the third man. I came back here to . . . to live and to wait."

If you could call this living, Decker thought. From what he could see his friend was simply surviving.

"Eat, there is plenty," Tomàs said. "Perhaps tonight so much will not go to waste."

Estralita always cooked more than enough, and it seemed that Tomàs had continued to do so in her absence.

"Tomàs, the ranch—"

"It is not a ranch anymore, my friend. No cattle, no horses. I stay here, that is all."

"Tomàs, this is no way to live."

"I wait for death, so I can go and join my beautiful Estralita."

Decker put down his fork and said, "So why not just end it yourself. Put a gun barrel in your mouth and pull the trigger."

Tomàs stared at Decker across the table, and then suddenly huge tears fell from his eyes. The man sobbed and put his head down in his arms. Decker waited uncomfortably, eating slowly.

Finally, Tomàs picked up his head and wiped his eyes with his sleeves.

"That is the—the first time I cried for her, Decker," he said, bitterly. "I could not before."

"Before crying would not have shamed you. If you expect me to pity you because you cried in front of me, you are mistaken."

"I want no pity."

"Then why did you wait for me to arrive before you cried? Eight months you've waited and when I arrive you cry. Why?"

"Perhaps you are right," Tomàs said. "Perhaps I am looking for pity."

"Well, don't look here."

Once Tomàs de la Vega had been a hunter of men, a lawman and then a bounty hunter. Then he met Estralita Gomez and fell in love. They settled here, and whenever Decker came to Mexico he stopped in on them.

They finished eating in silence, Decker wishing he had never come, never seen his friend like this.

"What brings you to Mexico now?" Tomàs asked.

"I'm hunting."

"Who?"

Decker told him, hoping that the questions indicated a possible change in Tomàs's attitude. If he was curious, maybe he was starting to come around.

"I have not seen such a man. He must not have come this way."

"Maybe he went by while you were drunk."

"I am drunk at night. During the day I am awake, and I hear everyone who goes by. I am waiting . . . waiting for the third man."

"You will grow old and die waiting."

"So be it."

After dinner they opened the bottle of tequila and drank directly from it, passing it back and forth.

"I will be leaving in the morning, Tomàs," Decker said. "Come with me."

"Why?"

"We can search better together than I can alone. I will be checking all the likely routes across the border. We can cover more ground together."

Tomàs stared at the bottle of tequila and shook his head.

"I must stay here."

"And rot?"

Tomàs shrugged.

When Decker went to sleep Tomàs was opening another bottle of tequila.

Amazingly, in the morning the man was awake and almost sober, even if he did look like death warmed over.

Once he was mounted Decker rode back to the house, where Tomàs stood in the doorway.

"Come with me, Tomàs."

"*Vaya con Dios*, my friend"

Tomàs de la Vega backed into the house and closed the door.

Decker felt very sad, and cursed Red Moran for bringing him to Mexico to see this.

Chapter Three

Red Moran rode into the town of San Louisa wondering if this time he would stay.

He had just under twenty thousand dollars in his saddlebags. He hadn't expected to find that much in the Pemberton Bank. He hadn't gotten that much from any three prior jobs combined.

Perhaps this was enough money.

Perhaps this was the time to settle down.

And perhaps not.

He had found San Louisa after his third bank robbery, and after the fourth had gone back there. After the fifth job he tried another town, didn't like it, and went back to San Louisa again.

The people of the small town knew and respected him, because he always came with money.

The women of the little town made themselves available to him for the same reason.

Red Moran knew they liked his money, but he flattered himself that maybe—just maybe—they would like him almost as much without money as with it.

The first to see him was old Roberto, the livery-man.

"Ah, señor Red, welcome back to San Louisa."

The old man's eyes shone for he knew that with Red Moran came many American dollars.

"Hello, Roberto. It's nice to be back."

"You will be staying?"

"For a while."

"Ah, good, good. I will take care of your horse."

"*Gracias*, Roberto."

Roberto watched hungrily as Moran reached into his pocket, came out with some coins and handed them to him. He closed his old hands over the gringo coins, enjoying their weight.

"Welcome back," Roberto said, "welcome."

"Thanks," Moran said. He took his saddlebags and rifle and left the livery.

The old man walked the horse inside, then anxiously opened his hand to count the money.

At the hotel Moran received the same greeting.

The owner of the hotel, Luis Hernandez, came out of his office and warmly shook Moran's hand.

"It has been much too long since your last visit, señor Red."

"I agree, Luis."

"Please, go to your room and rest yourself. I will have a bath drawn and a meal prepared."

"I knew I could count on you, Luis."

Hernandez watched eagerly as Moran put his hand in his pocket, came out with some coins and passed them over.

"It is our pleasure to serve you, señor, always."

"Are Carmen and Rosa still in town?"

"But of course. They would not leave San Louisa knowing that you would soon return. Which of them would you like to come to you first?"

Moran brought the two women's pictures into his mind. Carmen was a tall woman, big-breasted and long-legged, with long dark hair—if it was still long.

Rosa was also dark-haired, but she was smaller and slighter than Carmen, and had breasts like ripe peaches.

"Who can choose?" Moran said.

"I understand, señor," Luis said wisely. "I will send them both."

"*Gracias*, Luis."

"*Por nada*, señor, I assure you."

As Moran went back to his room—which was on the first floor of the adobe hotel and always kept ready for him—Hernandez went back into his office, opened his hand and gleefully counted the money.

When the gentle knock came at his door Moran knew that it was the two women he had requested. He answered with his gun in his hand anyway, for even in San Louisa it didn't hurt to be too careful.

"Señor Red," Carmen said when he opened the door, "how wonderful to see you again."

She came in and pressed herself up against him. He was bare-chested and he could feel her breasts through the thin blouse she was wearing as she mashed them against him. Already, her nipples were hard. She snaked a hand around his neck and kissed him openmouthed, then moved past him revealing Rosa standing in the hallway. He knew Carmen was already undressing behind him, but now his attention was on Rosa.

"Ah, señor Red," she said.

She was a neat little bundle, Rosa was. She came in and also pressed herself against him. Her breasts were small but very firm, and didn't mash as flat against him as Carmen's had. She also reached a hand behind his neck, but she had to pull him down to her level to kiss him, whereas Carmen was almost as tall as he was. Rosa's hot mouth devoured him, and then she too moved past him and began to undress.

He closed the door slowly, his gun still hidden behind his back, and by the time he turned around they were both delightfully naked.

He drank in the sight of them eagerly. Carmen's breasts were large and round, with brown nipples, sagging just slightly, but from their own weight and not due to age. After all, she was probably under twenty-five. Between her legs her pubic hair looked like a dark, tangled forest. Her thighs and legs were long and solid, and he marvelled at what a big girl she really was.

Rosa's breasts were small, like two delicious mouthfuls, the nipples a delicate pink. Her pubic hair was wispy, almost nonexistant, and barely hid her womanhood from view. She was like a doll, but Moran knew that she was much stronger than her size indicated. He'd learned that from spending time between her thighs.

"We hope you are not too tired after your long journey," Carmen said. Rosa nodded her head in agreement.

"No, ladies," he said, discreetly laying the gun on the dresser top, "in fact, after seeing the two of you, I'm not tired at all."

After both Carmen and Rosa had pleasantly exhausted him, Red Moran gave them both too much money and shooed them away.

"I need my rest, ladies."

"You are much man, señor Red," Carmen said.

"*Si, mucho*," Rosa agreed.

Both women went out into the hall and huddled together and counted their money.

Inside the room, reclining on the bed, Red Moran smiled. Two energetic, eager, sweet-tasting Mex women in one bed was almost too much for a man to expect.

But not too much for Red Moran to expect.

Not in this town.

These people really loved him.

This was the way to live.

Chapter Four

Decker felt them before he either saw or heard them.

He knew he was being watched.

He rode with his head facing forward, for he knew that when it suited them they would approach him.

He was checking the most widely travelled routes from the Rio Grande further into Mexico. Of course, the river could have been crossed in many places, but there were certain areas that were the easiest and best, and he was trying these first. If Red Moran had chosen some other point of entry, it would make picking up his trail that much more difficult.

Still, the hunt was the best part for Decker. It used to be the money, but Decker saved his money, unlike a lot of other bounty hunters he knew who spent it as fast as they earned it, and then had to hit the trail again.

Decker hunted maybe four or five times a year, because he thought nothing of spending two months on a man's trail.

He knew that Eddie Gorman, for instance, tracked at least twenty men a year, bringing in more than half of them. If he didn't have a definite trail after a week or two, Eddie just gave it up and went after other prey.

Joel Lansdale, on the other hand, spent eight months tracking Jeffrey Banks before he finally cornered him in Nacogdoches, Texas.

Decker was neither as impatient as Gorman nor as dedicated—or stubborn—as Lansdale.

They were both good men, though, there was no doubting that.

Now Decker could feel somebody's presence off to his right, and he allowed his eyes to flick off that way. Two men were riding towards him at a leisurely pace, as if they just happened to be crossing trails with him.

"Hey, amigo!" one of them called.

Decker reined in and waited, angling his horse so that he wouldn't have to fire across his body if it came to gunplay. Eventually, the two men reached him and stopped. It was unfortunate that, at the moment, they were staying close together.

A few miles further west, Gilberto and Raquel Diaz were leading a band of bandits at a slow crawl in an easterly direction.

"I think you sent the wrong two men ahead as scouts, brother," Raquel said for what seemed like the fourth time in the last five minutes.

Gilberto Diaz was thirty-six, a hawk-faced man who considered himself, at five nine, too short. He had huge shoulders and arms, and felt that he had to make up in strength and ferocity what he lacked in height.

Raquel Diaz was also five nine, but of course this was tall for a woman. She was full-breasted, with wild, untamed, dark hair that fell past her shoulders. Every man in the band lusted after her, and every man was too frightened of Gilberto to ever do anything about it. Raquel constantly teased them about it, showing off her body whenever possible.

"Raquel, I have told you that all of the men must do the the same jobs at one time or another. They take turns. It was simply Miguel and Santo's turn."

Raquel looked at her brother and said, "I still don't think you should have sent them together. Between them, they haven't the brain of a rattlesnake. If they see a likely victim, they'll strike without looking."

"So?" Gilberto said. "They are Diaz men, are they not? They should be worth any four normal men."

"Gilberto," she said, shaking her head, "you not only flatter them, you flatter yourself."

"Well, you can never be accused of that, can you, sister? Sometimes I think you wish you were leading these men yourself. You could do a better job that I, eh?"

Raquel knew she could, but she also knew better than to answer that question.

"Well," she said instead, with a sign, "what kind of trouble can they get into out here?"

* * *

They both wore wide sombreros and sported carefully trimmed mustaches and sideburns. They were both smiling, and one of them had one gold tooth on top, almost right in the center of his mouth. Both had worn gunbelts on their hips with equally worn-looking Colts. Decker was sure, however, that the Colts were in fine working order.

"Can I help you?" Decker asked.

"Perhaps it is we who can help you, señor," one of them said. "Is it possible that you are lost?"

"No," Decker said. "It's not possible at all. Now maybe I can help you boys?"

"*Si*, señor, if you would," Gold Tooth said. "Do you have any tobacco or whiskey?"

"I don't smoke," Decker lied, "and I don't carry whiskey." He did have cigars but he wasn't about to part with any of them.

Besides, tobacco and whiskey weren't what these two were after.

Decker's instincts told him that these would-be *bandidos* were alone at the moment but were probably part of a larger group.

"Well then," Gold Tooth said, "do you have any American money?"

"Oh, sure, I've got some of that."

"*Bueno*," said Gold Tooth, who was obviously the spokesman. "We would like some of that, then."

"How much?"

"Well," the man said with a wide smile, "all that you have, señor . . . *por favor.*"

"No."

"Oh, señor . . ." the man said, shaking his head

sadly as if that had not been what he wanted to hear at all.

"No," Decker said, again.

Gold Tooth clucked his tongue, as if Decker had now said something he should be ashamed of. The other man backed his horse up a few paces, as if he suddenly realized he shouldn't be so close to his compadre.

That's better, Decker thought.

"Señor, please, you are being insulting."

"Not yet," Decker said, "but I'll be getting there soon if you and your friend don't ride . . . now!"

"Ay-yay-yay-yay," Gold Tooth said, shaking his head at the gringo's folly.

His compadre was obviously watching Gold Tooth closely, for when the leader made his move for his gun, so did the other man.

Decker never even pulled his sawed-off, cut-down shotgun from its holster. He simply swiveled the holster up and fired that way. The cloud of double-o came out and spread just enough to catch both men. Had they remained side by side he might have missed one, but in moving back the second man had positioned himself not perfectly, but certainly more helpfully, giving the shot pattern time to spread. At the proper distance, a shotgun is simply a devastating weapon that not only kills, but disfigures and dismembers as well.

Gold Tooth caught most of the blast in his left arm and shoulder, and was torn from his horse while his arm was torn from his body. The second man was hit in the right shoulder, but the wound was not fatal.

Rather than fire the second barrel, Decker pulled his rifle from his scabbard, levered a round and fired, striking the second man square in the chest. He fell from his horse and landed hard on his back, but he never felt it.

Decker levered another round, dismounted and walked over to Gold Tooth. The man's arm was gone, and blood was pulsing from his shattered shoulder.

"Aye, señor, mercy," the man cried, blood foaming on his lips. "*Por favor*, señor."

The man would die soon enough, but Decker knew what the man was asking. He placed the barrel of the rifle against the man's forehead and fired.

Both of the Mexicans' horses had run off, but Decker decided there was probably nothing on them that he would have wanted. He ejected the spent shell from his shotgun, and replaced it with a live one. He then turned away from both men, remounted and rode off at a gallop.

If they were from a larger group, then no doubt someone would be along to check out the shots.

He didn't want to be around when they got there.

Chapter Five

The bandits led by Gilberto Diaz and his sister, Raquel, rode towards the sound of the shots and slowed only when they saw the bodies of the fallen men.

"Spread out," Diaz ordered.

He, Raquel and five other men rode towards the bodies while the other twenty men fanned out to see what they could find.

"Ramon," Diaz said.

While he scratched his unshaven face, Ramon Muniz dismounted and went to examine the men.

"They are both dead, Gilberto."

"I know that, fool! Check their guns!"

Ramon bent to check them, then straightened and asked, "Check them for what, *Jefe*?"

"*Stupido!* Check to see if they have been fired!"

Ramon nodded, bent and checked both men's guns and then stood up.

"They have not been fired, Gilberto. They are both still in their holsters."

"Miguel and Santos," Diaz said, staring down at

the two brothers who, until very recently—maybe fifteen minutes ago—had been members of his band. "They were good men."

"They were fools," Raquel said. "I told you not to send them together. They picked on the wrong person, Gilberto, and this is what they got for their trouble."

"They knew how to handle a gun," Gilberto said, looking at his sister, "and yet they were both killed before they could touch them."

"A better man," Raquel said, laughing. "One would not be hard to find."

"*Silencio.'*

Raquel fell silent, but a mocking smile remained on her lips. Ramon looked up at her, felt a rush of desire that knotted his stomach and heated his loins, then looked away before Gilberto could see.

"Shall we bury them, Gilberto?"

"No. Strip them of their guns and anything else they have of value."

While Ramon was doing that three of Diaz's men came riding up to them.

"Gilberto?"

"*Si.*"

"A trail, leading that way," one man said.

"How many men?"

"One."

"One man killed them," Diaz said, shaking his head in disgust.

"A better man," Raquel reminded them.

Gilberto threw her a murderous look, but did not say anything.

"Get the rest of the men," he told the three who

had just ridden up. "We will follow the trail and find out who this man is."

Gilberto and Raquel rode a bit further on, away from Ramon.

"From the wounds I would say a shotgun was used, and then a rifle," Raquel said.

"That much I knew from the sound of the shots," Gilberto said, scolding her for not knowing that herself. "We will find him."

"Gilberto, this is folly. Why follow this man just to see who he is?"

"He killed two of my men."

"Our men," she reminded him, "and we have better things to do than to track him."

"He killed two of our men, sister," Gilberto said. "That cannot go unpunished."

"Who will know?" she said, shrugging.

"*I* will know, and the men will know. We will find him and kill him."

Raquel made a disgusted sound and looked up into the sky, as if for divine guidance.

Ramon rode over to them and Gilberto asked, "Was anything taken from them?"

"Nothing, Gilberto."

"Ride ahead to my town and tell them we are coming. We will be hungry when we arrive."

"*Si*, Gilberto."

"Ramon," Raquel said.

"*Si?*" Ramon's throat went dry, as it always did when Raquel Diaz addressed him personally— which was not very often.

"Do not stop to rob any gringos, eh? You might pick on the wrong one."

Diaz gave his sister a hard look and waved at Ramon to go.

"Why do you say it was a gringo?"

"Mexicans do not use shotguns."

"Perhaps. Soon we will find out who your *better* man is," Gilberto said, "and see just how *much* better he is."

He did not see his sister's face when she smiled.

A day later Decker rode into a town that had no name posted anywhere. There had been no signpost, and there was no indication on any of the buildings. The hotel said simply "Hotel" and the cantina "Cantina," and so on.

A town with no name.

Eerie.

As he rode through he was almost given to believe that the town with no name also had no people, but then he caught a glimpse of someone in the cantina, and someone doing business in the general store. The streets, however, were virtually deserted, and it was only noon.

Strange.

He rode until he found the livery and then dismounted. Walking inside he called out, "Anyone here?"

He heard some movement and then a boy of about sixteen appeared.

"Señor?"

"I want to leave my horse."

"*Si*, señor," the boy said, bobbing his head and coming forward.

Decker handed him the reins of the dun.

"Rub him down and give him some feed."

"Will you be staying overnight, señor?"

"I don't know yet. I'll be staying at least long enough to get something to drink and eat—if it's to be had, that is. Where are all the people?"

With a shrug the boy said, "Inside, señor."

"Why are they inside."

The boy shrugged again and said, "It is hot."

"Hot," Decker said. "Sure. Look, take care of the horse, all right?"

"*Si*, señor."

The boy walked the horse further into the livery, and Decker left and walked over to the cantina. Not knowing whether or not he was staying overnight—and hoping that he wasn't—he had left his saddlebags and rifle on his saddle.

When he entered the cantina he saw that the boy had been at least partially right. There were about seven or eight men inside, some at the bar, some seated, all drinking. Besides them there was a sleepy-looking bartender and a bored-looking Mexican whore.

Decker approached the bar and said, "*Cerveza*."

"*Si*, señor," the bartender said, doing all he could to stifle a yawn.

The two men standing at the bar looked him up and down, and then looked away. The was a filthy mirror behind the bar and in it he could see the other men—two at one table, three at another, playing a lackluster game of poker—look his way, and then away.

The whore was sitting at a back table alone, her elbow on the table, her hand under her chin. She appeared to be young and, although somewhat plump, even a little pretty. When he got his beer he lifted the glass to her in a salute, which she barely acknowledged.

In most towns, she would have been all over him by now.

"Quiet town," he said to the bartender.

"*Si*, señor."

"Nobody outside."

"It is hot."

"You know, I've heard that."

"*Si*, señor."

"What's the name of this town?"

"The name, señor?"

"Yes, name. *Como se llama*."

"*Me llamo* Miguel."

"No, the town. What's the name of the town?"

For all the trips he'd made into Mexico, Decker had never been able to acquire even a working knowledge of the language. He knew how to order beer and food—as long as it was chicken—and ask somebody their name, but that was it.

"Señor, perhaps I can help?"

It was a man's voice, and Decker turned to see that one of the men had stood up from the poker game and walked over to him.

"Can you?"

"This town is very quiet, as you have observed, and it has no name."

"Why is that?"

The man shrugged and said, "There seems little need."

Decker didn't understand that.

"Well, you live here. If that's how you feel."

"We have little to say about it."

"Jose, you talk too much," the bartender said.

"Perhaps," Jose said, and went back to his poker game.

Decker turned to the bartender and said, "Any chance of getting something to eat?"

"*Si*, señor."

"Do I get a choice?"

"Tortillas."

"Good choice."

"Juanita!" the man shouted, and then rattled off something in Spanish. Decker assumed she was being told to get the food. Maybe he'd done her a disservice by assuming she was a whore. She was young enough to be the bartender's daughter, and maybe she was just a waitress.

Decker turned around with his beer in hand and looked at the table where the poker game was being played. The man, Jose, was gathering the cards up, getting ready to deal. The stakes looked small.

Decker walked over.

"Mind if I sit in for a few hands?"

The other men did not look up, but Jose did and said, "As you wish, señor."

Decker sat down and Jose dealt the cards, calling and dealing five-card stud.

Decker was dealt a king down and a queen up. Both were of the same suit, hearts.

One of the other men showed an ace, and started the betting with a dollar. Since the stakes were small and he was only playing to pass the time, Decker raised a dollar.

Jose dealt out the third card.

Decker got a ten of hearts, the man with the ace got another ace. For the first time Decker saw some emotion on someone's face as the man smiled.

The other man in the game had two small cards and Jose had a jack and a five.

The man with aces bet five dollars, and from the reaction Decker guessed that this was a substantial jump in the stakes—in his honor?

Jose called the bet, and Decker raised. The man with the two low cards folded, and the man with the aces raised again. Decker called after Jose, but decided that if he was going to stay in this hand he had trapped himself into bluffing.

Jose dealt out the fourth card and Decker drew a king. He now had a busted straight, but two kings. Aces were still high on the table. Jose was showing a pair of fives.

The aces bet five dollars, Jose called and Decker raised ten.

The man with aces swallowed.

"Did I raise too much?" Decker asked innocently.

"The raise is ten dollars, señor," Jose said. He looked at the other man as if to say, "You started it," and said, "What do you do, Silvio?"

Silvio examined his cards, swallowed again and then timidly raised five dollars.

Decker anticipated raising again when suddenly Jose said, "I raise twenty dollars."

Silvio made a sound and Jose gave him the same look he had given him moments before.

"I call," Decker said.

Silvio had no recourse but to call with his aces.

Jose dealt out the last card.

Decker got another king, giving him two on the table and one in the hole.

The aces didn't improve.

Jose got a third five.

Some hand, Decker marvelled. He had chosen the right moment to sit down.

Now the other men in the cantina moved towards the table to watch, including the bartender.

"It is my bet," Jose said.

He counted out his money and dropped it in the center of the table.

"Twenty-five dollars."

Decker counted out his money and tossed it in.

"I raise twenty-five."

"The bet is fifty," Jose said, looking at Silvio.

Silvio, who had obviously been winning while the game had been low stakes, counted his money.

"I–I do not have that much." He looked as if he were about to cry.

"How much do you have?" Decker asked.

Silvio counted again.

"Forty-four."

"That's the bet," Decker said. He reached into the pot and took six dollars back.

"I'll call," Jose said. "What do you have, señor?"

"Three kings," Decker said.

They both looked at Silvio, who mournfully turned over his cards to show two pair, aces and eights.

"I have three fives, señor," Jose said. "You are the winner."

"Thank you."

Decker raked in his money and Silvio stood up to leave. He had just lost in one hand what it had taken him two hours to win.

"Shall we continue?" Jose said, looking self-satisfied.

"I'm game," Decker said.

The third man, whose name Decker had not yet heard, nodded, and Decker picked up the cards to deal.

Chapter Six

Decker didn't take another hand in the next five, losing almost all of what he had won, and the girl came out to tell him that his food was ready.

"Would you gentlemen excuse me?"

"Of course," Jose said.

The excitement of that single hand of poker had quickly died and the mood in the place was once again sleepy.

Decker moved to an empty table and the girl brought out his food. The two men left at the table continued to play two-handed.

"Could I have another beer, please, Juanita?"

"*Si*, señor."

Up close he saw that she was very pretty indeed, in spite of her plumpness. She had smooth skin, large breasts, strong legs and she smelled clean. Decker remembered Miss Milly's stock in Pemberton, and thought that this girl would do very well there.

She brought him another beer and then went back to her table, where she had been sitting when he arrived, and took up her former position.

The sound of an approaching horse was oddly loud and everyone looked up when they heard it. Decker thought he saw a hint of fear in the bartender's eyes.

The horse stopped right in front of the cantina and a man entered moments later. He looked around, his eyes pausing for a moment on Decker, then walked to the bar.

"Gilberto is coming," he said to the bartender, who now did look frightened, as did most of the other men in the place. The only people who didn't seem to be affected by the news were Jose, the girl and Decker. "When he gets here he, his sister and the rest of the men will be hungry."

"Juanita!" the bartender shouted, his voice sounding abnormally high. "Did you hear? Gilberto and his sister are coming."

The girl very deliberately leaned over and spat on the floor.

The bartender said something to her in rapid Spanish and she finally stood up.

"Juanita," Decker called.

She looked at him and then came over to his table.

"Who is Gilberto?"

"The dog who thinks he owns this town," the girl said with distaste.

"Is that why the town has no name, and why the streets are empty?

"They are all afraid of him," Juanita said.

"I see."

"I must prepare some food. Perhaps I will grind some glass into it, as well."

"Well, I guess I'm lucky I got mine already, eh?"

She smiled at that, and her face became almost beautiful because of it.

"Señor, if I was you," she said, becoming serious, "I would finish eating and leave this town. Gilberto does not like gringos."

Decker looked down into his plate, which was still generously full, and decided he'd probably have to gulp his food down to do that.

"Your cooking is much too good to rush eating it, Juanita."

She grinned again, and stroked his face.

"You are a gringo fool, señor. I wish Gilberto was not coming, but—" she took her hand from his face regretfully and went into the kitchen.

"Ramon!"

The voice was Jose's, Decker saw, calling out to the man who had just entered.

"*Si*, Jose?"

"What kind of mood is the great Gilberto in? Should we hide our women and children?"

"You would be well advised to hold a civil tongue in your head, Jose. Gilberto is in a very bad mood."

"Why is that?"

"Someone killed two of our men, and Gilberto wants blood for blood."

Decker, chewed his food slowly and listened carefully.

"How did that happen?"

"Someone gunned them down with a shotgun before they could touch their guns," Ramon explained, "and then finished them with a rifle."

Decker washed down his mouthful with a swig of beer and wondered how many men this Gilberto had? He was obviously the leader of the bandit band that the two men he had killed belonged to.

"Is his sister with him?" Jose asked.

"Of course."

Jose looked over at Decker and said, "You are in for treat, señor. Raquel Diaz is the most beautiful woman in all Mexico."

"How interesting."

Ramon looked suspiciously from Jose to Decker, and then back again. It was time to leave.

"You will be very impressed—that is, if you stay long enough."

"Well," Decker said, looking regretfully at his plate, "I'm afraid I really have to be moving on."

Decker, not a man to frighten easily, knew that it would be prudent to be gone when Gilberto and his band arrived. He had started to stand when suddenly Ramon pulled his gun and pointed it at him.

"Stand very still, señor."

Decker did as he was told, cursing himself for not having been prepared for this. The man called Ramon had clearly seen that he was a stranger, but Decker had hoped to be able to leave before the man realized that that meant he was a good bet to be the man who killed the two bandits.

"That is a shotgun in your holster, is it not?" Ramon asked.

"That it is."

"I would ask you to keep your hand away from it, *por favor.*"

"Whatever you say."

"I think Gilberto will be very happy that you are here, señor."

"If you say so."

"Please, take your gun out with your left hand and drop it to the floor."

Decker did as he was told.

"Now, please sit and finish eating. Juanita is an excellent cook."

"Isn't that a coincidence," Decker said. "I was just telling her that."

Decker sat down, damning himself for a fool. His gun was on the floor and there seemed no sure way out of this short of charging the man and hoping he was a bad shot. He could upend the table, but the man was so much on edge that he might fire at a second's notice.

In light of the circumstances, Decker did the only thing he could.

He continued to eat.

Chapter Seven

While they were waiting for Gilberto and his men—not to mention his sister—to arrive, Juanita brought out a plate of food for Ramon. As she passed Decker on the way back to the kitchen she gave him a long look. She had obviously been trying to pass him some sort of message, but he was too dense to see what it was.

Ramon, holding his gun in his right hand, picked up a dripping tortilla and took a bite out of it. He chewed, keeping his eyes on Decker, continued to chew, with some difficulty, then swallowed . . .

And gagged.

Blood came from his mouth suddenly as he doubled over, dropping his gun. Decker was on his feet quickly, rushing towards him. He pushed Ramon away from his gun, but he needn't have bothered. He was past worrying about that. He staggered back, clutching his throat as blood continued to pour from his mouth, and then he fell over.

Decker picked up his gun and walked over to where Ramon was lying, Jose close behind him. Ramon was lying on his back, his eyes fluttering as blood oozed from his mouth.

"*Me Dios*," Jose whispered behind Decker. "What happened?"

Decker walked over to where Ramon's plate was and poked around in it with his finger. He came up with little bits of ground glass stuck to the tip of his index finger.

"Looks like Juanita added something to a recipe that already had some bite."

The bartender leaned over and said, "Glass?"

"Ground glass," Decker said, looking down at Ramon. "This fella's insides must be in pieces."

Ramon's eyes had rolled up into his head by now, and he was dead.

Juanita came out of the kitchen and walked over to Decker.

"Is he dead?"

"Thanks to you he's dead and I'm alive, Juanita. I'm much obliged."

"What have you done, girl?" the bartender demanded, holding his head in his hands.

"She saved my life, that's what she did."

"But she has forfeited all of ours," the man said. "The entire town."

"Paco is right, señor," Jose said. "Gilberto will now take his revenge against the whole town."

"I see."

"I do not care," Juanita said. "Señor, when you leave please take me with you."

"Juanita!"

She shouted something at him in Spanish, during which Decker heard her call him "Papa."

In English she said, "I am ashamed of you, and ashamed of everyone in this town. You continue to let Gilberto and his *bandidos* frighten you. Well, he does not frighten me."

"Foolish girl," her father said.

"Señor . . ." she said to Decker.

"Maybe the girl is right," Decker said, looking at Paco, Jose and the other men in the saloon. "Maybe it's time for this town to stand up for itself."

"Señor," Jose said, "if we do that, will you stand with us?"

Me and my big mouth, Decker thought. He had a trail to pick up, but then Juanita had done him a big favor, and maybe he owed it to her to help them.

"All right, Jose," Decker said. "If you can get enough men with guns who are willing to fight, I'll stand with you."

Jose grinned.

"Señor, I think I can do that." He turned to the other men in the room, said something to them in Spanish, and they all stood up and nodded.

"This is a start, señor, and before we are done we will have many more men, as well."

"Then get to it," Decker said. "We don't know how far behind this fella the rest of them are."

As Jose and the rest of the men left, dragging the dead man with them, Juanita came over and pressed her breasts against Decker's arm.

"Señor, how can I help?"

"Well, I'll tell you, Juanita," Decker said, nudging Ramon's plate. "Maybe you could just fix up a big batch of these here tortillas—you know, the ones with the *big bite* in them?"

"It will be a pleasure, señor."

Chapter Eight

Red Moran liked Mexican food almost as much as he liked Mexican women. That was why he figured that when he settled down for good, it would be down here, in Mexico.

He was in the cantina, finishing up some chicken and rice with beans when Carmen, the big-breasted whore, entered, obviously looking for him.

"Ah, señor Red," she said, smiling when she saw him.

"Carmen. Sit yourself down, sweetheart."

She sat opposite him. She was wearing a very low-cut peasant blouse and was giving him a good look at her swollen breasts. Her nipples were pressing against the blouse.

"I wanted to tell you how happy I was that you are back, señor Red, but last night . . . well, last night Rosa was there, too."

"I thought you two were friends."

"Oh, we are friends," she said, "very good friends, señor Red—but even with a friend one does not wish to share a man such as yourself."

Moran smiled.

"I know what you mean," he said. "You're both beautiful, but being in bed with both of you a man doesn't know where to look first."

"And so?" she said, grinning. "Now that we are alone, you would know where to look?"

"I would know where to look," he said, leaning forward, peering down her blouse, "and where to touch."

"Are you . . . finished eating, señor Red?"

"I am finished, Carmen."

They both stood up and walked up to his room together.

The bartender was clearing the table when Rosa came storming in.

"Raul, have you seen Rosa?"

"*Si.*"

"Where?"

The bartender simply looked up at Moran's room and continued clearing the table.

"*Puta!*" Rosa snapped, which was an odd thing for a whore to call a whore.

She stormed up the stairs angrily, vowing to pull Carmen's hair out by the roots for trying to get more of Red Moran's money for herself.

The bartender paused long enough to watch her climb the steps, skirt swirling around her marvellous calves, and then went into the kitchen. From there, he would not hear the noise when the two cats began to fight over the mouse.

Gilberto Diaz, Raquel and their men were riding to Gilberto's town at a fairly leisurely pace.

"I hope Ramon has Juanita cook up a big batch of tortillas," Gilberto said to Raquel.

"That is all she is good for, that one," Raquel said. "Cooking."

"That is all she is good for as far as you are concerned," Gilberto said, smiling. "I can find other uses for little Juanita."

"She is fat," Raquel spat, "like a cow."

"She is a comfortable woman, that one. Teats like pillows, and thighs like—"

"I do not wish to hear this!" Raquel snapped.

"And you?" he asked. "Will you let a man come near you and touch you?"

"When I find a man who deserves me."

"Hah! With the high opinion you have of yourself, you would think you were a queen."

"I am a queen," she said, raising her chin. "Queen of the *bandidos*."

"I am the king of the *bandidos*," Gilberto pointed out, and you are my sister. That does not make you a queen, *mi hermana*."

"To be your queen a woman would have to be married to you," Raquel said, "and I would not wish that on any woman."

Gilberto threw his sister an admiring glance. She had proud firm breasts and long legs. If she were not his sister . . . and perhaps, soon, that would not be enough to matter.

But now, his thoughts were of Juanita.

"My little Juanita will have a feast for me," he said with a leer.

Raquel looked at her brother and thought brutally, I hope she bits your *cojones* off!

Chapter Nine

True to his word, Jose returned with more men with guns, but as Decker counted, he saw that they were going to come up some short.

Outside the saloon, with the men standing in the street waiting for instructions, he spoke to Jose.

"Jose, how many men would you say Gilberto has?"

Jose rubbed his jaw and said, "Twenty-five, señor, perhaps more."

"How many more?"

"No more than thirty."

"We have fifteen," Decker said, looking at the men in the street.

Jose's face fell.

"We cannot do it, señor?"

The worried look on his face was so pathetic that Decker reached out and patted the man on the shoulder reassuringly.

"Oh, we'll do it, Jose. We just have to figure out the right way."

"You will figure that out, señor, will you not?" Jose asked with a big smile.

"I'm sure going to give it a try, Jose," Decker said. "We'll give it one helluva try."

Sometime later, Decker, Jose and three other men arrived at the cantina with saws and hammers in their hands.

"What are you going to do?" Paco asked, eyeing them with great concern.

"We are going to make some small adjustments to your establishment, Paco," Decker said.

The men walked past him and went up the steps to the second floor.

"What do you mean, adjustments?"

"Nothing that will damage your cantina, Paco— at least, nothing that can't be fixed later," Decker said, trying to soothe the man.

Juanita came out from the kitchen and moved behind the bar, next to her father.

"Is everything ready in the kitchen, Juanita?" Decker asked.

"Everything is ready, señor Decker."

"Aiee, I do not like this," Paco said, putting his head in his hands.

"Please, Papa," she said, "señor Decker knows what he is doing."

"Perhaps," Paco said, "but I do not think I know what I am doing."

"You're pouring drinks, Paco, like always," Decker said, "just pouring drinks."

Chapter Ten

The *bandidos* rode into town, their horses crowding the empty streets.

"Why do we keep coming here?" Raquel asked aloud. "This is a nothing of a town."

"It is my town," Gilberto said, "that is why we come."

When they had first discovered the town it had been called Little Cross. When Gilberto saw that there was no law—and no backbone in the townspeople—he decided to adopt the town as his own. He pulled down the "Little Cross" sign and called it "his" town from then on.

That had been several months ago.

"We should find a better place to hole up," Raquel complained. "In the mountains would be better."

"Ah, but in the mountains there would be no Juanita," her brother said.

"Any whore can give you what she gives you. Besides, if you like her that much you could take her with you."

That didn't sound like such a bad idea to Gilberto, but he didn't tell his sister that.

Gilberto stopped in front of the canteen and shouted orders for three men to take the horses over to the livery. He said the rest of the men were free to come inside and eat or do whatever they wanted. Since there was nothing else to do in the town but eat, the men followed Gilberto and Raquel into the saloon.

Decker figured that with as many horses as the *bandidos* had, more that one man would have to take them to the livery. He took Jose with him and they waited there, while the rest of the men took their places as he had directed them.

A lookout had passed the word that the *bandidos* were coming, so when the three men showed up with the horses, it was no surprise.

Except for them.

The horses were herded into the corral behind the livery, and then the three men walked through the stable to get to the other side.

As they entered Jose clubbed one of them over the head with his gun, while Decker did the same on the other side of the door. The third man, who had been walking between the other two, froze and stared into Decker's gun.

Jose came up behind him and put him to sleep, too.

"All right, quickly," Decker said. "Let's tie them up and see what's happened in the saloon."

* * *

What was happening in the saloon was that the *bandidos* had taken every table, and the men without tables were standing at the bar.

"Drinks for all my men, Paco!" Gilberto shouted, slamming his hand down on the table.

"*Si*, señor."

Gilberto sat at one table with Raquel while his men crowded at the others, and the bar.

"Where is my Juanita, Paco?" he demanded, loudly.

"She is getting the food ready."

"That's my good girl," Gilberto said. "She knows how to treat her man."

Raquel made a noise and looked away.

Juanita heard the light knock on the door and opened it hurriedly. When Decker entered he saw that her hands were shaking.

"Don't get nervous on me now, Juanita," he said, taking her hands in his. "I need you."

"I will be fine."

"How's the food coming?"

"It is almost ready."

"Good."

Decker could hear a man's voice shouting from the other room.

"Is that him?"

"That is him."

"He's got a big mouth, hasn't he?"

She smiled nervously and said, "Yes, he has a very big mouth."

* * *

"Where is Ramon?" Gilberto shouted.

Behind the bar Paco froze, and wondered if he had cleaned the blood off the floor well enough.

"I sent Ramon ahead!" Gilberto yelled. "Where is he?"

Paco's bottom lip quivered, and his hands shook . . .

From the kitchen Decker could feel it. He could feel Paco's hand shaking.

"Get out there," Decker said to Juanita, giving her a little push.

"What do I say?"

Decker told her . . .

"Where is Ramon?" Gilberto asked again.

At that moment Juanita came out of the kitchen, just as Paco was about to crumble.

"There is my Juanita," Gilberto said, putting his arms out.

Juanita came over and allowed him to put his arms around her waist and rub his face in her bosom.

"Mmm," he said, "she is always the cleanest woman I have ever smelled."

"That's because you always smell so dirty," Raquel said.

"And you?" Gilberto asked.

"I," Raquel said, giving Juanita a nasty look, "am going to the hotel to take a bath."

Raquel got up and walked out, followed by the eyes of every man in the place, even the frightened Paco. Her jeans were so tight they showed her heart-shaped behind flow up into her thin waist.

"Ah, Juanita, did you miss me?" Gilberto asked.

"*Si*, Gilberto," Juanita said without enthusiasm, "I missed you."

"Perhaps you can tell me, eh?"

"Tell you what?"

"Where is Ramon?" Gilberto asked, his tone puzzled. "I sent him on ahead."

"He was here," Juanita said. "How do you think I knew to put on an extra pot of food?"

"Well then where is he?"

"He is at the hotel."

"What is he doing there?

Juanita gave Gilberto a reproachful look and said, "Papa hired a new girl, and Ramon decided to try her out."

"Ah, that Ramon," Gilberto said, moving his hand down from her waist to cup her behind. "Is she very pretty, this new girl?"

"Pretty enough."

"But not as pretty as you, eh, my Juanita?"

"No, Gilberto," Juanita said, "not as pretty as me. Will you let me go now so I can bring out the food? Your men look hungry."

"I will release you now," Gilberto said, letting her go, "but after we eat will be another matter, eh?"

" 'Yes," Juanita said, "it will be another matter, Gilberto."

Chapter Eleven

Juanita went back into the kitchen and collapsed against Decker's chest. He put his arms around her, extremely conscious of her plump breasts crushed against his chest.

"You did fine, Juanita, just fine."

"Raquel, she went to the hotel. She will know that Ramon is not there."

"She left before you told him that," Decker said. "Don't worry, this will all be over soon. Come on, you've got to add the last ingredient to the food."

Next to the stove, on the floor, was a pile of what looked like salt, only it wasn't. It had taken a lot of glasses to make that particular pile of "salt."

"Come on, spoon it in," Decker said, aware that he was telling her to do something that would kill most of the thirty men out there, all of whom he did not know. Still, he knew that if they had the chance, they would gladly kill him.

He'd do anything to avoid that.

Juanita called Paco in to help her serve the food.

"You've got to go as fast as you can and get as

many of these plates served before someone bites into theirs. Do you understand?"

"We should have more people."

"Have you had more people in the past?"

"No."

"Then they'd be suspicious if you did now, wouldn't they?"

"One more wouldn't hurt," Juanita said, and she looked so frightened that Decker gave in, hoping it wouldn't blow the whole deal.

"All right, get me an apron and introduce me as . . . as John—if anyone asks."

They got him an apron. He took off his gunbelt, tucked his gun into his belt, and put the apron on over it.

"How many can you carry?" Juanita asked.

"How many can you?"

"Six?"

"Jesus," he said, "give me four."

She balanced four on his arms, two each, and then she and Paco took six apiece. That made sixteen, and there were plenty more men out there who wouldn't get any if someone started eating too fast.

Should have thought of that before, Decker thought. He could have had Juanita put out empty plates, and then one main dish in the center of each table. That way they would have had more of a chance of getting a maximum number of *bandidos* before they realized something was wrong.

It was too late now. He knew which one was Gilberto, and that's who he'd take out first when things started going.

"Let's go."

They went out with their plates and started dol-ing them out. The *bandidos*, fresh from the trail, were all drinking beer or whiskey, and Juanita had time to go back into the kitchen and get some more plates, handing a couple quickly to Decker. Some of the men at the bar caught Paco and asked for more drinks.

They got twenty plates served before Gilberto looked suspiciously at Decker.

"Juanita!"

"*Si?*"

"Who is this?"

Juanita looked at Decker, who had stopped on his way back to the kitchen.

"Uh, that is John. We hired him to help out."

"When?"

"Uh, yesterday."

"He does not look like a waiter," Gilberto said, looking at Decker's boots, "and he does not dress like a waiter."

Suddenly, the bandit leader saw the bulge be-neath Decker's apron.

"And he carries a gun? Come here—" Gilberto started, and he began to rise when suddenly there was a scream, followed by another.

Gilberto turned in the direction of the scream and saw that several of his men were yelling, clutch-ing at their throats, or bleeding from the mouth.

"What—"

He grabbed for his gun, not knowing what was going on but knowing something was wrong, and that Decker was no waiter.

Decker went for his gun, but the hammer caught on the apron. Gilberto fired, striking Decker in the left shoulder. Decker spun with the impact, pulled his gun free and fired at Gilberto, hitting him in the right arm. The bandit's hand opened and he dropped his gun.

Above them several newly sawed hatches in the ceiling opened and men began to fire down into the crowd of bandits. The men at the bar drew their guns, but two men with shotguns entered by the front batwing doors, and three came in from the back, led by Jose. They all fired both barrels, shredding the men at the bar to pieces.

Decker was down on one knee, firing his gun at any man he could see who wasn't bleeding from the mouth.

Gilberto was on the floor, groping for his gun with his left hand. Juanita came up behind him and hit him over the head with a plate of tortillas. A bullet struck her then, and she went down.

"Juanita!" Paco shouted. He came out from behind the bar and a bullet struck him in the leg.

Decker regained his feet, tucking his empty gun into his belt. The apron had been discarded. He bent over and retrieved Gilberto's gun and started firing again.

By the time the bandits realized that they were being shot at from above, it was too late. Each man at a hatch had a pistol and a rifle, so they could fire without reloading. Only one man from above was shot, and fell through the hatch to the floor.

It took less than a minute, and then silence fell over the cantina. White smoke curled up and floated near the ceiling, where heads were poking out to see if it was all over.

Decker walked among the fallen bandits. Many of them had been shot, and some of them were simply lying on the floor, bleeding profusely from the mouth.

Decker dropped Gilberto's gun and took out his own, reloading as he checked the bodies.

"Is it over, señor?" one man asked from the ceiling.

"It's over," he said. "You better come down and check your dead."

"Juanita!" Decker heard Paco call.

He turned and saw the man crawling towards the girl, his hand trying to stem the blood that was leaking from his thigh.

Decker rushed over and turned Juanita over. The bullet seemed to have passed right through her shoulder. Her eyes fluttered open and she moaned in pain.

"Easy," he told her.

"Am I going to die?" she asked.

"No," he said, brushing her hair out of her eyes, "you are not going to die."

She saw the blood coming from his shoulder.

"Are you going to die?"

"No, and neither is Paco."

Paco reached her and took her hand.

"How is Gilberto?"

Decker looked at the bandit, who was just beginning to stir.

"He's got your tortillas on his head, but he's not going to die, either."

"Give me a gun and I will kill him," she said.

"Now, you just lie still here with Paco."

Three of the men who had been upstairs came downstairs now.

"Watch him," he said, pointing to Gilberto, "and collect all the guns from the floor. I don't want anyone to wake up and start shooting."

The two men who had come in the front door moved forward to help, and Decker stood up.

"Where are you going?"

"There's still one more."

Juanita winced at the pain in her shoulder, but said, "Raquel. She went to the hotel."

"She must have heard the shooting."

"I'll get her. Is there a doctor in this town?"

"*Si*," Paco said, "and if he heard the shooting he will be hiding under his desk."

"Tell me where his office is and I'll bring him back with me."

Paco gave him directions and he left, first for the hotel, and then for the doctor.

Chapter Twelve

Raquel Diaz was luxuriating in a hot tub at the hotel, her hand idly rubbing herself between her legs, when she heard the shooting.

Her brother and his filthy men, shooting up the town again. You would think that since he claimed the town for himself he wouldn't want to damage it, but he was probably drunk already.

She leaned back and ran her hand up over her belly and began to stroke her breasts. It had been a while since she'd had a man. Raquel teased the men she rode with, but she never slept with any of them. That would have cost her some of their respect, and she needed to maintain that. It was alright for Gilberto to eat and drink—and whore—with their men, but Raquel had to keep her distance. She had to get her men elsewhere, and rarely did she ever sleep with one twice. Even if she wanted to, she had either moved on—or killed them.

Decker entered the hotel and asked the clerk where the baths were. The man nervously eyed

Decker's wound and stammered as he replied, giving directions.

"In the b–back, señor," the man said, "b–but the lady is t–taking a—"

"I know what the lady is doing."

Decker walked down to the end of a hall and kicked the door open.

The woman in the tub stood up abruptly, water running off the glorious curves of her body. She reached for her gun, which was hanging on a chair next to the tub.

"Hold it!"

She stopped, bent over at the waist, large breasts dangling. This woman had the most beautiful body Decker had ever seen.

"Gringo?"

"That's right."

"Was it you who killed our two men?"

"Yes, but they tried to kill me."

"There is no need to explain. They were fools. You were a better man, eh?"

"Yes."

"And the shooting at the saloon?"

"The people of this town decided they didn't like the idea of your brother claiming it."

She nodded.

"May I straighten up?"

"Please do."

Even with the wound in his shoulder hurting, Decker couldn't help but react to this woman, and she knew it. She could make a dead man stand up and salute.

"May I know your name?"

"Decker."

"I am Raquel Diaz."

"A pleasure."

The ends of her hair were damp and they stuck to her shoulders and breasts. She ran one hand over both breasts, then brought the other one up so she could palm both of them and flick the nipples.

"There is plenty of water in the tub, señor Decker," she said, "and it would do your wound good."

"I'm afraid I'm going to have to ask you to get dressed and come with me."

"Shall I dry off first?"

"If you like."

She stepped from the tub and he watched while she dried herself with a towel lovingly, taking a long time to do it, performing for him. He watched every move, regretting that at the moment he could do nothing about it, but watching with a certain amount of real pleasure. He had been on the trail for some time now, and seeing a woman, especially one as beautiful as this one, was a treat.

When she was dressed she stood facing him, hands on hips, and said, "My compliments, señor."

"Why?"

"Any other man would have broken by now."

"Broken?"

"Men have begged for me, señor."

"I'm sure many men have broken, señorita, and with good reason."

"*Gracias*," she said, graciously accepting the compliment. "Perhaps another time?"

"I hope so."

She started to reach for her gun and he said, "Ah–ah, leave it there."

She smiled, raised her hands in surrender, and walked towards him. He backed away so she could come out into the hall, and that close to her he saw that she was almost as tall as he was. The skin of her face was brown, but flawless, without blemish—as was the flesh of her body.

"Tell me, señor. Did the townspeople ask you to help them do away with us?"

"No. I just happened along."

"Our luck, eh?"

"I guess."

They walked the rest of the way through the hotel in silence.

"We have to stop for the doctor," he said when they were on the street.

"My brother?"

"He's alive," he assured her. "He's got a bump on his head, but he's alive."

"From his little Juanita?"

"Yes."

The woman laughed, an honest, hearty laugh that came from deep inside of her. It made chills run through him, and his groin ached.

"It serves him right," she said when her laughter had subsided. "What of the rest of the men?"

"Most of them are dead, I'm afraid."

"Oh, don't apologize," she said, waving a hand negligently. "I think I was ready to stop being a *bandido* queen, anyway."

They stepped down from the boardwalk to the street and Decker started walking back towards the saloon.

"Señor Decker?"

Pointing the other way she said, "The doctor's office is in this direction."

He stared at her, then simply said, "Thank you."

"*Por nada.*"

Walking behind Raquel Diaz all the way to the doctor's office was an experience in itself. It made Decker wonder if he hadn't made a mistake in not taking her up on her offer in the bath.

When would there be another like it?

Raquel Diaz was having thoughts along similar lines. She was sorry that Decker had not joined her in the bath. She still needed a man, and Decker certainly attracted her.

She would have liked to sleep with him before killing him.

Chapter Thirteen

Moran had not enjoyed the fight. He could think of better things to watch two women do than fight, even if they were fighting over him.

When the fight had started he decided to pick up his clothes and leave, so he didn't know what the outcome had been. Rosa had anger on her side, but Carmen had size and weight. He wondered if this meant that he was going to have to choose between the two of them.

Maybe there was a new girl in town, but if there were she'd have to really be special to take his interest away from Carmen and Rosa.

Moran walked around the town, checking to see if it had changed since he'd been gone. He was glad to see that it hadn't. There was no sign of progress, anyway.

Progress meant more people, and if more people started coming into San Louisa, he'd have to stop coming here.

"Señor Moran!"

He turned and saw the mayor, Eduardo Felipe,

walking towards him. The mayor was a bandy-legged little man with a pencil-thin mustache who bowed and smiled a lot. He remained mayor because no one else wanted the position.

"Hello, Mayor."

"Señor, I have a huge favor to ask of you."

"What's that, Mayor?"

"You have come to San Louisa at just the right time, señor Moran."

"Why is that?"

"We have had a problem here in the past few weeks, and I know you will be able to help us. You are obviously a very capable man, señor."

"Mayor," Moran said, "could you get to the point, please?"

"The point? Ah yes, the point. Ah, we here in San Louisa find ourselves in dire need of a sheriff."

"A sheriff?" Moran repeated, wanting to be sure that he had heard correctly.

"*Si*, señor. A sheriff—ah, the man with the star . . . on his chest? Am I not saying it correctly?"

"And you want me—" Moran said, laughing now.

"*Si*, señor," the mayor said, puffing his chest out. "As mayor of San Louisa I ask if you would accept an appointment as sheriff . . .

"Señor . . . ?

"Why are you laughing, señor . . . ?

"Did I say something funny?"

Moran couldn't answer. This was so funny,

so ironic, that as soon as he *could* answer—as soon as he could stop laughing—he was going to accept.

Sheriff Red Moran, of San Louisa, Mexico.

Chapter Fourteen

The doctor pronounced twenty-three of the *bandidos* dead, and three so badly injured they probably would not last the night. There were the three from the livery, who were thrown in jail, and Gilberto, who was patched up and tossed in jail with them. Raquel was given the second cell in the two-cell jailhouse.

"If you want me, señor" she told Decker seductively as he put her in her cell, "just come and get me."

"That's very tempting," he admitted.

The doctor had bandaged his shoulder wound—which was not as bad as Juanita's—and announced that both Juanita and her father would survive.

One of the townsmen had been killed, and one injured.

Decker found Jose sitting behind the desk in the sheriff's office. He hung the cell keys on a hook on the wall.

"You have a sheriff's office, but no sheriff?" he asked.

"Well, to tell you the truth," Jose said, opening a drawer, "before Gilberto and his men . . . adopted . . . this town, I was the sheriff."

To illustrate his point he took a sheriff's star out of the drawer and pinned it to his chest.

"You gave us back our town, señor, and for that we thank you."

"Why didn't you do it before?"

"We needed a leader."

"You were the sheriff."

"Ah, yes, but I was never a leader, señor. I knew that. If Gilberto ever thought I was, he would have killed me."

"So now you're the sheriff again."

Smiling, Jose said, "Thanks to you."

"I get the feelin' I was used, Jose, and I don't like it."

"Señor? I do not understand?"

"Never mind. Enjoy your town."

"Señor Decker."

"What?" Decker asked at the door.

"Wouldn't you like to stay with us—at least until your wound heals?"

"My wound will heal fine in the saddle. I've got a man to find."

"A man?"

"That's right. That's my business, just like yours was taking care of your town—only I take care of my own business . . . Sheriff."

"I am sorry I do not meet with your approval, señor. Perhaps I can help you. Who is this man you seek?"

"His name is Moran."

"I do not know the name. Perhaps if you described him for me?"

Decker did, giving the description that was on the poster, and then he showed Jose the poster.

"Ah, of course. I know this man!"

"You know him?"

"Well, I saw him."

"When?"

"A week or so ago. He passed through here, stayed for one night."

"This man?" Decker asked, tapping the poster while it was still in Jose's hand. "You're sure."

"He ate over at the cantina. Even played poker with us. You can ask Paco and Juanita."

"I will," Decker said, taking the poster back. "Which way did he go when he left?"

"He continued south."

Well, at least he had a definite direction in which to go, now.

"Will you be staying in town for the night at least?" Jose asked.

His shoulder wound was hurting, but he didn't want Jose to know that.

"I might as well give my horse a night's rest."

"I will tell the clerk at the hotel that you are not to be charged for the night. The same for the livery."

"Thanks a lot."

"It is the least we can do, señor. After all, you did give us back our town."

Yeah, Decker thought, until the next *bandido* comes along and asks for it.

Chapter Fifteen

Decker went to the cantina and found Paco back behind the bar, limping back and forth as he attempted to clean the mess of broken glass behind it. Decker could hear it crunching beneath the man's feet.

"Paco, you should be off your feet."

"And who will take care of by business?" Paco asked, frowning unhappily. "Look at this mess. Glass, broken wood, and holes in my ceiling . . ."

He gave Decker a look that said it was all his fault. Maybe having his town back wasn't worth the mess his cantina was in.

Indeed, the place was a shambles. Pieces of broken tables and broken glass littered the floors. And something would have to be done about the square hatches Decker'd had the men saw in the floors of the rooms above.

"What about your neighbors? Won't they help you clean up?"

"They are all off somewhere getting drunk, bragging about how they killed twenty *bandidos* each, so that they won't have to help me."

"This town is really a great place to live, isn't it, Paco?"

Paco scowled and did not answer.

"Where is Juanita?"

"Upstairs in her room."

"May I go and see her?"

"*Si*, the second door on the right is hers."

Decker went upstairs, found the door and knocked.

"Come in."

He entered and Juanita smiled from the bed.

"I knew you would come."

"How are you feeling?"

"Fine," she said, but he knew she was lying.

"That's good," he said, "because my shoulder hurts like hell."

She smiled and said, "Yes, so does mine. Will you be staying the night?"

"Yes. The sheriff has extended to me the hospitality of the hotel."

"No, you will stay here with us."

"That's all right—"

"I insist—and later, during the night, when father is asleep, you can come to me."

"Come to you?"

"We will make love, no?"

He smiled at her and said, "With the two of us toting these bad shoulders around?"

"We will manage."

"Juanita—"

"You do not want me because you know Gilberto has had me," she said, sadly.

He sat on the bed and said, "That isn't it at all."

"Then why?"

"I wouldn't do that under your father's roof."

"We can go somewhere—"

"You will stay right in that bed, young lady."

"Then we will not make love?"

"I'm afraid not," he said, and then added, "not this time."

She brightened.

"When you come back this way?"

"Perhaps," he said, "when I've finished my job."

"And by then we will both be healed."

"Yes."

"And we will make wild, passionate love."

He grinned at her enthusiasm and said, "We will see. Right now I think I'll earn my keep by going downstairs and helping your father clean up."

"You will be leaving in the morning?"

"Yes."

"Will you come and say goodbye first?"

"I'll be leaving early."

"Wake me."

"All right," he said, "I'll wake you. Get some rest, now."

Decker went downstairs and offered to help Paco clean up, an offer Paco accepted with his customary frown.

Turning in for the night Decker found himself thinking not of Juanita down the hall, but of Raquel Diaz, sitting in a jail cell.

"If you want me," she had said, "come and get me."

What a waste.

Chapter Sixteen

As the new sheriff of San Louisa, Red Moran had the run of the town even more than he had before, if that was even possible.

He moved out of the hotel and into the sheriff's office, but still intended to use the hotel room for visits with certain citizens.

All of his meals were offered to him for free, as were his drinks, but he continued to pay for them, anyway. It pleased him to do so, and he knew that the townspeople liked his money. Maybe, if he started taking advantage of his new position, they wouldn't be so happy to have him anymore.

Eventually, he found out something that he had been wondering about: whether or not San Louisa had any new whores in town. Well, he found out in a big way. One of them—a fiery redhead from Texas—caught his eye because he was from Texas, too.

Suddenly, he wasn't so convinced that the best-looking, best-feeling, best-tasting women came from Mexico.

Carmen and Rosa didn't like that at all.

The redhead's name was Crystal, and she was only too happy to service the new sheriff of San Louisa who, she had heard, paid very well.

"I have to tell you one thing," Red Moran said, watching Crystal get dressed.

"What?" she asked, smiling.

"You really are going to make it hard for the Mexican gals in this town to make a living."

"That's a sweet thing to say," she said, sliding her second stocking up her long leg.

Her pale skin, red hair and green eyes made her the only whore in town that didn't have dark hair and skin.

"What brought you here from Texas?" he asked.

"I rubbed somebody the wrong way."

"Who?"

"The wife of a wealthy rancher. She said if I ever showed my face in Texas again she'd shave my—well, I just better not, that's all."

She slid her shoes on and stood up.

"So what brought you here?" she asked.

"I come here from time to time. I like it. It's quieter that the United States."

"Yeah, but maybe too quiet. Now that you're the sheriff, though, will you be staying longer?"

"That depends."

"On what?"

"On how long you're staying?"

She grinned, walked to the dresser and took the money he had left there for her.

"Ooh, thanks," she said, after counting it. "I almost feel as if I haven't earned it."

"Believe me," he said, "you have—and there's more where that came from."

"You could make a girl stick around longer than she intended," Crystal said. "See you later."

"Count on it."

When Crystal left the hotel it was just getting dark. She started walking to the rooming house in which she was staying.

There was an idea rolling around in her head, one that would take her smarts and Red Moran's money—if he was telling the truth about there being more of it.

As she passed an alley two girls jumped out and grabbed her, dragging her in.

In the alley she turned to face Carmen and Rosa.

"It is time for you to leave town, *puta*," Carmen said in a menacing tone.

"That's an odd thing for you to be calling me," Crystal said, indicating that she had some understanding of Spanish. "Tell me why it's time for me to leave."

"It is bad enough we had to share señor Red's mon—bed with each other," she said, catching herself just in time, "we do not intend to share him with you." Rosa was trying to match Carmen's tone, but her voice was just too small and high to pull it off.

"You don't, huh? Well, now, that's really funny," Crystal replied.

"Why is it funny?" Rosa asked, looking confused.

"Well, I wasn't intending to share him—or his money—with either one of you, either."

"Take our advice," Carmen said.

"Leave town," Rosa added.

"Forget it," Crystal said, moving to walk past them.

Carmen moved to block her path and Crystal swung her fist and hit the larger woman in the stomach. The blow was unexpected, and Carmen folded up, fighting for air. Crystal turned to face Rosa then, who backed off, her hands held up in front of her.

"When your friend gets her breath back tell her—and the other girls in this town—that you all better be nice to me from now on." Crystal marched to the mouth of the alley, then turned and added, "You'll all be working for me, soon. Wait and see!"

Crystal left the alley, knowing that she had just taken a big step towards achieving her goal, the one she had set for herself when she first arrived in town.

All she needed now was Red Moran's money.

Which, considering her considerable charms and talents, should be easy enough to get her hands on.

Chapter Seventeen

In the morning Decker entered Juanita's room but decided not to wake her. He leaned over, kissed her on the forehead and left.

"She will be very angry with you," Paco said as he came downstairs.

"Tell her I couldn't bear to wake her."

"I will tell her."

The place looked considerably cleaner since Decker had swept out all the wreckage and righted the tables. He had even thrown out the batch of food that had been mixed with the ground glass and cleaned out the pot.

Decker went to the livery, collected his horse and paid the kid.

"Oh no, señor. The sheriff he say—"

"Keep it, son."

"*Gracias*, señor.'

Decker mounted up and rode out of town—whatever the hell name they were going to pin on it next—and his only regret about his decision to leave it behind him and never return was the disappointment that would cause Juanita.

Still, the whole town made him sick because he knew that the next gunman or *bandido* who came along with a few men to back him up could have the town for the asking.

They deserved whatever they got.

Chapter Eighteen

That same afternoon Jose heard Raquel calling him from her cell. Since he'd been thinking about her ever since they had put her in the cell, he got up and hurried back.

"It's very hot, Jose," she complained. Her shirt was open and he could see her breasts very clearly. They were large and firm and they glistened with her sweat. A large knot formed in his throat.

"I am sorry—"

"Please, if I could just have a bath—"

"That would mean I would have to take you over to the hotel."

"Well, you are the sheriff, are you not?"

"Yes."

"Then you can do it if you like."

She came right close up against him so that the bars were all that separated them.

"And since we will be at the hotel anyway, with all those beds." She lowered her voice and whispered, "I have not had a man in a long time."

Jose backed away quickly, banged into the wall,

hurried out to get the cell key, and then came back in and unlocked her cell.

"I will have to stay with you while you take your bath," he warned.

She smiled at him, ran her finger along his jaw-line and said, "I would not have it any other way."

It was two hours later when she finally returned with the cell keys. Although bedding the sheriff had successfully scratched the itch she'd been feeling, she was sorry that it had not been Decker, instead.

"It took you long enough," Gilberto complained as she unlocked his cell.

"I had to wait until I was in bed with him to catch him off guard," she said innocently.

"Sure, you just had to see what he had inside his pants before you killed him, eh?"

Gilberto came out of the cell, followed by his other three men.

They all went out into the office and found their guns. Raquel had used the sheriff's own weapon to kill him. He had been totally unaware of what was happening, because she chose the very moment he had climaxed to pull the trigger. She felt that this was probably a fine way for a man to die.

"What do we do first?" Raquel asked. "Teach the town a lesson?"

"To hell with this town," Gilberto said, strapping on his gun. "I want that bastard gringo! I want to hang him up by his balls."

"I would like to see that," Raquel said.

"I am sure, little sister, that you would—and you will get your chance."

They left the jailhouse by the back door, went to the livery, killed the boy who worked there and took their horses.

Decker was trailing Red Moran.

And Gilberto and Raquel Diaz were trailing Decker.

After Decker had left the home of his friend, Tomàs de la Vega, the Mexican had continued to drink. He drank until he ran out of whiskey, and when he sobered up he thought of some of the things Decker had said to him.

He didn't like them.

He packed a few of his things into his saddlebags, went outside and saddled his horse, then left the horse a safe distance fron the house. That done, he very methodically set fire to the house where he had lived with his beautiful wife, walking around it with a torch, making sure that it would burn evenly and completely.

That done he put out the torch and stood back to examine his handiwork. He watched it burn for a while, then turned and mounted his horse. He rode away and did not look back once. As he was riding away he wondered just how far ahead of him Decker was.

In his past, most men would have died on the spot for the things Decker had said to him, but Decker was his friend, and had said those things out of friendship. Of this Tomàs was very sure.

When he found him, however, he still owed him at least a punch in the nose.

Tomàs de la Vega was moving back among the living.

Chapter Nineteen

"You want to do what?" Red Moran asked Crystal.

"I want to open a real high-class cathouse, right here in San Louisa."

"That's crazy," he said, laughing.

They were together in his bed at the hotel, she lying on her back and he sitting up.

"Why?"

"This is a little, sleepy town. I wouldn't want to see it change."

"Maybe the people who live here all the time would feel different. Maybe they'd want it not only to change, but to grow. Did you ever think about that?"

"No," he admitted. "I don't usually think beyond what I want."

"Look, Red," she said, sitting up and putting her hand on his left arm, "we've only known each other less than a week, now, but I think we're two of a kind."

"Both from Texas?"

"More that that. I think that maybe whatever money you've got you didn't get . . . playing fair."

"That's a good way of putting it."

"But look at the position we're in? You're the law here, and you're probably also the richest man in the town."

"That ain't sayin' much," he said, "not in this town, anyway."

"Hear me out. I would already have two pretty good girls working for me—Carmen and Rosa."

"If you could keep them from fighting."

"They only fight over you, and they don't even do that anymore."

"Not since you came along."

"We could get us a few more girls and build us a nice little business. Whaddya say, Red? Your money and my . . . talent?"

Red rubbed his jaw and while he did Crystal's hand slid down and began to rub something else of his.

"Cut that out," he said, slapping her hand away. "I can't think if you do that."

"Sorry."

"Don't think you're gonna sweet talk me into this, Crystal. If I go for this it will be because it's a good deal—and because we meet my conditions."

"What conditions?"

"Well," he said, thoughtfully, "for one thing, I don't think the town has to necessarily benefit from this operation of yours."

"What do you mean? We'd benefit and the town wouldn't?"

"I'd like to keep the town just the way it is, and to tell you the truth, I don't think they'd much mind."

"So we'd take in all the profits, and the town would stay *out of the action*?"

"We wouldn't have to let everybody know about the place," Red Moran said, "just certain people."

"People with money to spend."

"Right."

"On women."

"Right."

"Then . . . we're partners?"

"That depends," Moran said.

"On what?"

"On how much you need to set this thing up."

"Well, I could buy that old rooming house I'm staying in real cheap, get some of the locals to come in and fix it up for me real cheap . . . I guess I don't really need all that much."

"How much is not all that much?"

She told him.

"By golly," he said, breathing a sigh of relief, "I think I can swing that."

I'll bet you can, Crystal thought, pushing him down on the bed, *and I'll just bet there's a lot more where that came from.*

"Now wait a minute, wait a minute," Moran said, pushing her away.

"What?"

"Before we get all tangled up here there's just one more thing we need to talk about."

"Crystal's."

"What?"

"You were gonna say that we need to talk about the name of the place."

"That's right."

"I've already got a name," she said. "Crystal's."

"Why Crystal's?"

"Because even though we'll be using your money, honey, we're gonna have to use my name."

"Why?"

"Would you want to go to a whorehouse called 'Red's' or 'Moran's'?"

"I guess not."

"Besides, if you didn't get that money by fair means, you don't really want to advertise the fact that you're down here in Mexico, do you?"

"Why not? The law can't touch me."

"But a bounty hunter might."

He frowned. A bounty hunter! He hadn't really considered that possibility.

"They wouldn't put a big enough price on me for a bounty hunter to want to come all the way down here."

"I wouldn't know, sweetie. I don't know what you did, but it still seems to me we're better off calling it Crystal's. Has sort of a ring to it, doesn't it?"

"Yeah, I suppose it does."

"Then we have a deal?"

"We have a deal."

He put his hand out for her to shake and she said, "You gotta be kidding," and pushed him back down on the bed.

Chapter Twenty

"What do you mean 'we lost him'?" Raquel demanded. "We have been following his trail for better than four days, how could we lose him?"

"I am not a trailsman," Gilberto said, testily. "I have sent Juan, Martinez and Orlando on ahead to try and pick up the trail again."

"Ha!" she laughed, derisively. "We will be lucky if they can find their way back to us."

"Raquel, there are times—"

"Just remember the times that I have gotten you out of jail, my brother, and forget about all the other times. If it wasn't for me, you would be sitting in a jail cell right this minute."

That was hard to argue with, so Gilberto simply sat and sulked.

When they were alone there was an amazing switch in personalities. In the company of their *bandido* band there would never have been any question that Gilberto was the dominant sibling, but if anyone had ever seen them alone there would have been no doubt that Raquel dominated him. Although Gilberto was the older by almost five years, it had been Raquel who had brought her older brother up after their parents died.

It was Raquel who was taking charge now.

"We will stop studying the ground in vain and simply travel south. We should be able to find out whether he has passed through the next town or not."

"And then?"

"And then the town after that!" she snapped, testily. "We will find him, 'berto, and then you can play big tough *bandido* leader again—unless some chubby *puta* pushes herself in your face again."

"Raquel . . ." Gilberto said, feebly.

Sometimes Raquel thought that her brother should have perished in the same fire that claimed their parents. They might both have been better off.

Chapter Twenty-one

The uncomfortable feeling of being followed was gone, for the first time in four days.

Decker's hunter's instinct had been telling him that while hunting he might have also somehow become the hunted. It could have been another band of bandits, or it could have been Gilberto and his sister, somehow escaped from jail. Now, however, after four days, the feeling was gone, and he didn't miss it at all.

There was a signpost up ahead announcing a town called *Rio del Gato*, or River of the Cat. There was also the scent of water strong in the air, and when Decker finally came within sight of the town he stared in surprise.

Rio del Gato was a fairly large town as adobe towns went, and it seemed to have been built right along the shores of a large lake. Decker frowned, for it seemed an odd location for a lake, but then he had never really been this way before.

He rode down to the town and along the main street, and the smell of the lake was strong, fresh and clean. He sure couldn't argue with that. He'd been in enough foul-smelling towns to appreciate the scent of this one.

He'd passed through three small towns in the past four days where Red Moran had been recognized, so he knew he was on the right track. This town was the most appealing by far, as far as he was concerned. He wondered how appealing it would be to a man whose saddlebags were bulging with money.

The entire town seemed to be made up of adobe buildings, including the livery stable, which looked as if it might have once been a church.

A woman with a face so weathered and leathery that her age couldn't be guessed came out of the livery to meet him.

Decker dismounted and handed her the reins.

"How long will you be staying, señor?"

Decker looked at the sky and saw that it was late afternoon.

"Perhaps the night. Rub him down good and feed him."

"*Si*, señor, but if I may say so . . ."

"Yeah?"

"This *caballo*, he looks like he could use several days' rest."

Decker cast a critical eye over the animal and saw that he did indeed look worn.

"Do you have any horses for sale?"

"*Si*, señor, in the corral on the back."

"Then perhaps I'll be back to talk to you about one."

"At your leisure, señor."

Decker took his saddlebags and rifle from his

saddle. The lateness of the day and the probability of having to haggle over a horse made him decide that he would indeed be spending the night.

He asked for and received directions to the hotel, which was a two-story adobe structure to which a wooded porch had been added. As he approached it a man stood up from a straight-backed wooden chair and greeted him.

"*Buenos tardes*, señor."

"Afternoon. Are you in charge here?"

"*Si*, señor. I am Emilio. You are looking for a room?"

"I am."

"We have several."

"Do you have one from where I'd be able to see the lake?" Decker asked.

"But of course, señor. This way, please."

Decker followed the man inside, where the clerk presented him with the hotel register. Decker put his saddlebags and rifle down and signed in, then checked the names for the past two weeks. He had to go back half a week further than that before he found Red Moran's name. He'd lost several days on Moran, then, and would surely need a fresh horse in order to pick up the pace.

Moran was apparently so confident that no one would follow him into Mexico that he had no qualms about signing his real name in the book.

Idly, Decker wondered if Moran even knew that the bank manager had died?

"*Gracias*, señor," the clerk said, accepting the book back. He was a tall, elegant-looking man in sweaty, faded clothes that had probably once been elegant, as well. A fallen aristocrat, perhaps.

"Here is your key, señor."

"*Gracias.*"

"You would perhaps like a bath?"

"I would love a bath."

"We take the water directly from the lake. It has amazing soothing properties."

Although the man spoke English slowly and precisely, he did not speak with a very heavy accent. He had probably spent a lot of time in the United States at one point in his life.

"I will have the bath ready within the half-hour?" the man asked.

"Fifteen minutes would be better."

"*Muy bien.* Fifteen minutes, then."

"Tell me, Emilio."

"*Si?*"

"Do you have a sheriff in this town?"

"Oh, *si*, señor. Doesn't every town have a sheriff?"

"Not *every* town."

"We have a very good sheriff, señor. He is Ernesto, my cousin."

"I see."

"But even though he is of my blood, I can still say with conviction, señor, that he is a very good sheriff."

"I'm sure he is, Emilio. I'll be down for that bath."

"*Si*, señor. It will be ready."

Decker picked up his saddlebags and rifle and

walked upstairs. He dropped his gear on the bed and walked to the window which overlooked the main street and afforded a perfect view of the lake.

He wondered what the Spanish word was for lake, and why they hadn't used that in the name of the town. Did *rio* mean lake as well as river?

He rubbed his hand over his face and thought about Red Moran. If the man had been covering his trail it probably wouldn't have taken Decker this long to track him. The man was travelling openly, without fear, and was staying well ahead of him.

His shoulder wound throbbed, and he realized that if it hadn't been for the incident during which he'd received it, he might be further along than he was. He didn't like to admit it, but the wound had slowed him down for a couple of days, until he had consciously picked up the pace.

He took a clean shirt from his saddlebags and went downstairs to get that bath.

Decker cried out when the clerk poured the water over his head.

When the clerk told Decker they took the water right from the lake, Decker had assumed that the water would be heated up.

"That's cold!"

"*Si*, señor," the clerk said, grinning. "It feels good, does it not?"

Decker was about to reply sharply when he realized that it *did* feel good. His pores were opening up and he felt refreshed. Why was he paying thirty-five cents for this when he could have jumped in the lake himself—and washed his clothes in the progress?

"You got any soap?"

"*Si*, señor."

The clerk handed him the soap and Decker said, "I think I can handle it now."

"Oh, yes, of course, señor. Please, enjoy your bath."

"Thank you."

Decker lit a cigar and did that for nearly fifteen minutes, getting up once to dump a second bucket of water that the clerk had left behind over his own head. It was not as cold as the first had been, but it did the job.

Decker was just about to rise and get out of the tub when the door to the room opened and a man walked in.

The man was tall and slender, and he wore a fancy sombrero with little cloth balls hanging from the brim. Around his lean hips he wore two pearl-handled Colts that looked ludicrous—as did the man himself. His gunbelt was festooned with fancy silverwork, and he stood with his thumbs hooked into the belt, staring at Decker.

He had one other piece of silver on his person.

A badge, which betrayed the fact that he was the sheriff.

"Señor," the man said, "we must talk."

Chapter Twenty-two

"Talk about what, Sheriff?"

The man walked towards the tub, and Decker saw that he moved with an exaggerated swagger.

"I am the sheriff of this town, señor."

"Yes, I know," Decker said, staring at the man over his cigar, still not sure he was seeing what he was seeing. "You're Emilio's cousin, Ernesto."

"Sheriff Ernesto," the man said, "that is, Sheriff Ernesto Garcia."

"It's nice to meet you, Sheriff."

"Señor," the man said, trying his best to look important, "we must talk."

"So you said," Decker replied. He took the cigar out of his mouth and asked, "Do you mind if I get out of this tub? The water is getting tepid."

"No, of course not," the sheriff said.

"Could you hand me that towel?"

The sheriff glared at the towel, because to hand it to Decker he would have to unhook one of his thumbs from his belt, and he practiced that pose every day.

"Of course," he muttered. He used his right hand, gave Decker the towel, and then jammed his thumb back into his gunbelt.

Decker got out of the tub and began to dry himself off.

"Well, Sheriff?"

"Señor?"

"You said we had to talk."

"*Si*, señor. My cousin, Emilio, tells me that you were very interested in the hotel register when you checked in."

"Your cousin, Emilio, is very observant."

"*Si*, señor, like me."

"I'm sure."

"Señor," Garcia said, scowling, "I must ask you what you business in Rio del Gato is."

"That's a fair question, Sheriff, and it deserves a fair answer."

"I am glad you see it that way."

"I'm just passing through."

"Just . . . passing through?" the sheriff said, obviously expecting more. "On your way to where, señor?"

"I'm not sure."

"You are not sure where you are going?"

"That's right."

Garcia had a well groomed, full mustache, and he unhooked one of his thumbs so that he could stroke it, then replaced the thumb.

"Excuse me, señor, but that sounds rather odd to me."

"I'm sure it does, Sheriff."

Decker pulled his pants on, then took Moran's poster out of his pocket and handed it to the man.

"I'm looking for this man."

Garcia had to unhook both thumbs to accept the poster and unfold it.

"Red Moran," he read, and then his eyes widened as he continued, "bank robbery and . . . murder!"

"That's right."

"This man," Garcia said, "he was in my town?"

"He was."

"Señor," he said, holding his heart, "I am mortified, I am embarrassed, I am wounded . . . señor, *you* are wounded."

Now that Decker was out of the tub Garcia had noticed his shoulder wound.

"Did this man do that to you?"

"No, I got this from somebody else."

"Señor, you lead a very dangerous life. Are you perhaps a man of the law?"

"I am a bounty hunter."

"Ah, I have heard of such men. And this bounty you seek is this . . ." Garcia checked the poster. "Two thousand five hundred dollars?"

"That's right."

"And this man was in my town?"

"He was, two and a half weeks ago."

"*Santa Maria!*"

"Could I have my poster back, please?"

"Oh, *si*, señor."

Twenty-five hundred dollars was a lot of money

to anyone, but especially to a sheriff with delusions of grandeur in a small Mexican town.

Decker got dressed with the sheriff watching. As he strapped on his gun he asked, "Is there something else I can do for you, Sheriff?"

"Uh, no, señor."

All of the man's swagger was gone now and he was slouching.

"I apologize for having interrupted your bath."

"That's all right, Sheriff," Decker said, finding himself feeling sorry for the ridiculous-looking lawman. "You were just doing your job."

That seemed little consolation to the man as he slunk out of the room.

Undoubtedly, the man was thinking of all the silver ornaments he could have bought with twenty-five hundred dollars.

As Decker came into the hotel lobby Emilio gave him a sheepish look.

"Señor, I hope you did not mind—"

"That's all right, Emilio. Your cousin was right, you are very observant."

"*Gracias*, señor. I was the sheriff before my cousin got the job."

"And what did he do before he was sheriff?"

Emilio smiled and said, "He ran this hotel."

"That figures. Where's a good place to eat, Emilio?"

"The cantina down the street, señor. Excellent tortillas."

Decker closed his eyes. He didn't think he ever

wanted to eat another tortilla. He'd keep seeing those *bandidos* clutching their throats and slumping to the floor.

"I hope they can make something else."

"Oh, *si*, señor. They have a very wonderful cook. Roberta. She is—"

"Your cousin?"

Looking sheepish Emilio said, "*Si*, señor."

"I hope she was never sheriff."

"No, señor," he said, "Ernesto beat her by one vote in the last election."

"One vote, eh? Listen, Emilio, can you do me a favor?"

"Of course, señor."

"Take a look at this."

Decker took out the poster on Moran and passed it over to him.

"Do you recognize that man?"

Emilio studied the drawing closely and then shook his head.

"I am sorry, no, señor."

"He stayed in the hotel about two and a half weeks ago. His name is John Moran, but he signed in as Red Moran."

"I am sorry, señor," Emilio said, passing the poster back. "I do not remember him."

"Okay, thanks," Decker said. He folded the poster back up, tucked it in his pocket and started to leave.

As Decker started to leave Emilio called out, "Excuse me, señor?"

"Yes?"

"I was just wondering, señor," Emilio said,

"this evening, would you be wanting any . . . female companionship?"

"If I do," Decker said, "I'll arrange it for myself, Emilio."

"Of course. Please, enjoy your meal."

Chapter Twenty-three

After dinner—enchiladas and rice—Decker went over to the livery to talk to the leathery-faced woman about a horse. She took him out back to show him what she had.

There were three horses in the corral.

"Is this all you have?" he asked.

"I have three horses, señor," she said. "That is two more than anyone else in town."

"Jesus," Decker said, "I'm surprised you aren't the mayor."

"My cousin is the mayor."

He stared at her, then ducked underneath the corral fence to look over the horses.

There was a bay mare that was too heavy, a rangy roan and a small pinto with bowed tendons. The roan was the best of the lot, with no apparent infirmities.

"How much for the roan?"

"One hundred."

"That's crazy," Decker said. "I'll keep the horse I've got."

"That horse will drop dead if you ride him another twenty miles."

"Then I'll walk," Decker said. "I'd rather walk than pay a hundred dollars for that roan. How much for the mare?"

"A hundred dollars."

"She's overweight."

"Ninety dollars."

"How much do I get off for the pinto's bowed tendons?"

"The pinto is seventy-five—"

"Forget it. I'll give you my horse and twenty-five dollars for the roan."

She shook her head.

All through the dickering the expression on her face never changed. By the time they were done Decker had the roan for thirty-five dollars, his horse, and five of his cigars. He had decided that the woman was over fifty.

That done he took a walk by the water. While he was there a woman and a little boy came along, and the woman watched the boy play in the shallow water.

She appeared to be about thirty or so, pretty, big-bosomed and wide-hipped. Some men would say she was built for childbearing.

Decker figured she was built for making love.

He walked over to where she was sitting and said, "That's a fine-looking boy."

"Thank you."

She pushed some hair out of her face and looked up at him.

"How old is he?"

"Five."

"Is he yours?"

"He is my son."

"What's his name?"

"Ricardo."

"Named after his father?"

"His father had no name," she said. "His father was a gringo who rode into town and rode out again. I never saw him again."

"I'm . . . sorry," Decker said, awkwardly.

The woman had hiked her skirt up to get some sun on her legs, and he stared at her strong thighs and calves.

"Would you mind if I sat?" he asked.

"The sun will be going down very soon."

"That's all right. I'm not here for the sun."

She stared at him and he hoped that hadn't sounded to her the way it had to him.

"Sit, then."

He sat in the sand next to her.

"Why are you here?"

"In town?"

She shrugged.

"I'm here by the water for the peace and quiet, I guess. I'm justing passing through town. Why do they call this lake Rio del Gato?"

"The lake is called the river of the cat because years ago there was a big cougar who liked to come and drink from it."

"That's all he did? Just come and drink?"

"Yes. After they built the town someone saw

the cat one day, but all he did was drink and leave. Soon, the cat would come to the lake even if people were around, drink and then leave."

"He was gentle, then?"

"Yes."

"What happened to him?"

"Somebody shot him."

"What happened then?"

"The cat's body was thrown into the water, and now some people believe that his spirit lives on, protecting the town."

"Has it protected the town?"

She shrugged again.

"We have never had any trouble with *bandidos*, or bad men of any kind."

Decker figured it sure wasn't the town sheriff that was keeping them away, so maybe there was something to be said for the spirit of the cat.

"They also say that the water has healing properties."

"How true is that?"

She looked at him and said, "No one gets sick in Rio del Gato."

"Is that the name of the town, too, then?"

"It is all known as 'the River of the Cat.' I have also heard some gringos call the town 'Cat River.'"

"This is a lake, though."

She shrugged, as if that had very little to do with anything.

"Are you staying at the hotel?"

"Yes."

"Are you lonely?" She looked at him and he

saw that she had very big, dark, liquid-looking eyes—or was the lake reflecting off of them?

"Not . . . lonely, exactly."

He had turned down two women in the past week, plump and pretty Juanita and the beautiful Raquel. Both would have been trouble of their own kind.

This one would be no trouble.

They agreed that she would come to his hotel room after eight.

"I must find someone to babysit for Ricardo."

"All right."

"The sun is going down," she said, standing up. "Ricardo!" She shouted something in Spanish and the boy waved and ran out of the water. Decker saw that he had no shoes on, and his pants were rolled up over his ankles.

"Hello, Ricardo."

The boy did not answer him. The woman got up, took the boy's hand and walked away.

Decker watched her until she was out of sight, then took off his boots and rolled his pants up over his ankles.

He spent a couple of hours showing the poster around, but there was no one in town who re-membered seeing Red Moran, and yet his name was in the register.

All right, so he *had* been there. Even though no one had seen him, he'd been there and Decker was on the right trail.

He went to the saloon for a drink, then walked back to his hotel.

"How did you enjoy the food, señor Decker?" Emilio asked from behind the desk.

"The food? Oh, the food was fine, Emilio, just fine. *Gracias.*"

"Will you be leaving in the morning?"

"Yes, early in the morning."

"Have a good night, señor."

The tone of Emilio's voice and the look on his face told Decker that the woman from the beach had kept her appointment.

It was after eight o'clock.

In the morning the woman was gone, and so was the money he had left out for her. She had been very quiet when she arrived, very eager in bed, and then quiet again afterward. He figured she'd use the money to buy little Ricardo a new pair of shoes or something.

Decker got up to dress and was surprised to find that his shoulder was not bothering him very much today. Could it have been the water from the lake?

That was silly.

He finished dressing and went downstairs to pay his bill.

"We hope you have enjoyed your stay, señor," Emilio said, smiling broadly.

"It was interesting, especially the stories I heard about the lake."

"Yes, about the cat. It is nonsense, really, but some people believe it."

"Well, people have to have something to believe in."

"Come back again, señor."

It had been an interesting stay, but somehow Decker didn't think he'd be returning.

He walked to the livery where the woman had the roan saddled and ready for him. With a fresh horse under him he hoped to be able to catch up with Moran within two weeks, especially if the man had found a town he wanted to hole up in. It was Decker's theory that if the man came to Mexico after every job, then he must be coming to the same town. In all probability, it would be a small town that would not attract a lot of people, or attention. All Decker had to do was find that town.

When he left the town he rode along the water's edge for as long as he could, and when the waterline turned away he continued on.

There was something about the cat's spirit being in the water that made him uncomfortable.

He wondered what had happened to the man who shot the cat?

Chapter Twenty-four

When Gilberto and Raquel Diaz reached Rio del Gato, they discovered that they were four days behind Decker.

They realized this when they saw his name in the register.

They asked about him at the hotel, and were told by Emilio that he was a "very nice gringo."

At the livery, they were told that he bought a new horse, a roan, and "practically stole it."

They also heard the stories about the lake and thought it was nonsense.

Ernesto was in Raquel's room when there was a knock on the door. When Gilberto opened the door and saw the "sheriff" he started laughing.

Ernesto, confused, looked down at himself and then asked, "Pardon, señor, are you laughing at me?"

"You are the only one standing there in that ridiculous outfit, aren't you?" Gilberto asked.

"What ridiculous . . . ?"

"Is that badge for real?" Gilberto asked, touching the star on Ernesto's chest.

Ernesto backed away from the touch and said, "Please, señor. I am the sheriff."

"Raquel, look what we have here," Gilberto said, standing to the side. "The sheriff of this silly town."

Raquel came to the door and Ernesto's eyes popped at the sight of her. His cousin, Emilio, had been right. This woman was a beauty!

"Señorita—"

"This is my sister Raquel, Mr. Sheriff," Gilberto said, correcting any wrong assumptions the man might have made about them being in the same room.

"I beg your pardon, señorita—" Ernesto said, executing a bow.

"What can we do for you, Sheriff?" Raquel asked.

"I, uh—" The sight of Raquel had reduced Ernesto to stammers and stutters.

"Is it not clear?" Gilberto asked. "The sheriff heard you were here, sister, and came to have a look."

"Is that true, Sheriff?" Raquel asked, giving him an innocent look that started his heart pounding. "Did you come here to see me?"

"I, uh, well, the clerk downstairs, he is my cousin—"

"Maybe you could help us, Sheriff," Gilberto said.

"*Si*, señor, it would be my honor to help the señorita—uh, to help you."

"We're looking for a friend of ours."

"What is his name?"

"Decker."

"Oh, señor Decker. Yes, he was here—uh, four days ago, I think."

"Yes, that is what it indicated on the register downstairs."

"Then, how may I help you, señor?"

"Did he say where he was going?"

"You are friends of his?"

Raquel moved closed to the sheriff and said suggestively, "Señor Decker and I are very special friends."

"Truly?" Ernesto said, eyes wide.

"Yes, truly."

"*Did* he say where he was going?" Gilberto asked again.

Ernesto looked around as if someone might hear them and then said in a low voice, "He said he was looking for a man with a price on his head."

"How much of a price?"

"Two thousand five hundred American dollars."

"And the man's name?"

"Moran, Red Moran. I would never forget that name." It was indelibly etched in Ernesto's mind.

"Señor Decker is a bounty hunter?" Gilberto said.

Raquel looked at him and shrugged.

Ernesto, for all his fascination with Raquel, suddenly became a sheriff again, and frowning suspiciously, looked at them both.

"If you and señor Decker are such special friends, as you have said, why is it you did not know he was a bounty hunter?" he asked.

Raquel looked at Gilberto, who simply shrugged.

"I think we had better leave instead of staying overnight," he said, ignoring the sheriff. "We still have some daylight and can camp on the trail."

"Agreed."

"We can find the others in the cantina."

They picked up their gear and pushed past Ernesto into the hall. He watched helplessly as they went downstairs leaving him standing there, and then his pride began to sting and he went after them.

Downstairs he found Emilio in an agitated state.

"What is wrong?"

"Those two left," Emilio said indignantly, "and refused to pay for their room."

"They went to the cantina," Ernesto said, hitching up his gunbelt. "I will go and confront them. I do not believe they are what they pretend to be."

In the cantina Gilberto and Raquel found their three men and told them they were leaving.

"I would like a drink before we go," Raquel said.

Gilberto agreed, and they were sitting at a table with a beer in front of them when Ernesto entered. The other three men were standing at the bar.

"Señor, I must speak with you," Ernesto announced.

"Not now," Gilberto said.

"Señor, I must insist."

Gilberto looked at the sheriff, and then at his men, who were looking Ernesto up and down in disbelief.

"Look, Sheriff—if you really are the sheriff—I do not have time for you now."

"Señor, I am in authority here—"

Raquel stood up and Ernesto stopped talking as she faced him.

"Look, be a very good boy and go away, all right?" she said sweetly. "Otherwise you might get hurt—or worse yet, your silver might get dirty."

The three men at the bar laughed, as did even the bartender.

"Impossible," the sheriff said, firmly, "no one gets hurt here. The spirit of the cat would not allow it."

"That story of the cat again," Gilberto said, shaking his head and looking at his sister. "The clerk told us about that. It is utter nonsense."

"Please, señor, do not speak so of the spirit. You will anger it."

"Look," Gilberto said, standing up. The man was truly beginning to annoy him, and besides that, the wound in his thigh was throbbing. "My sister has asked you nicely to go away. So go away!"

"Señor, I am the law here! I must insist that you answer some questions."

"I think I am tired of you," Gilberto said. He took out his gun and pointed it at the sheriff.

"Put that gun away," Ernesto said officiously. "It will do you no good here."

"Gilberto," Raquel said, "let's leave this place."

"In a moment."

"Now!" She turned and jerked her head at the three men at the bar. They put their drinks down and left.

"Gilberto—"

"First I want this idiot's badge," her brother said. "I want to make him eat it." He tapped the sheriff's badge with his gun and said, "Take off the badge, fool."

"I cannot," Ernesto said, looking shocked. "I am the law."

"No," Gilberto said, putting the gun against the sheriff's forehead, "this says I am the law. Give me that badge."

"Gilberto, this man is crazed," Raquel said. "He is mad. He truly believes that the spirit of the cat will protect him from harm."

"Then I must prove him wrong."

With that Gilberto Diaz pulled the trigger. The hammer fell with a click, but there was no shot.

Gilberto's eyes flicked to his sister, who was staring at the gun in his hand.

"Raquel—"

"Gilberto, let's go! This place is cursed!"

Gilberto was tempted to pull the trigger again, but decided against it. Once could have been a misfire. Twice would be . . .

"Let's go!" he said.

He took the gun away from the sheriff's head and they hurried out. Their men had brought their horses around, and they mounted up and couldn't ride out of Rio del Gato fast enough.

When Tomàs de la Vega entered Rio del Gato he did so quietly, without fanfare. He spent one day, eating, drinking, listening.

He heard from the liverywoman of the stranger

who drove a hard bargain and "stole" a horse from her.

He heard about the incident in the saloon, when the town sheriff—a ridiculous-looking fellow—had stood up to a band of bandits and run them out of town. A lie, he thought, but then he also heard about the bounty that Decker was hunting, and he realized that the *bandidos* knew about it, too.

As for the story of the cat in the lake, he thought it was a pleasant diversion.

That night, as he went to sleep in his hotel room, he was convinced that trouble was stalking his amigo, Decker. From here on in Tomàs would have to travel much faster, with fewer stops, if he was going to get to Decker in time to be of some help.

In time to keep him alive.

He would not allow someone else who was close to him to die.

Chapter Twenty-five

In less that a week Crystal's Palace was set up and in business.

Moran and Crystal had purchased the rooming house Crystal was staying in and had used some carpenters from the town to fix it up the way they wanted. When they received the cloth they ordered, they'd be able to hang colored draperies and cover the furniture to match.

The first two girls they hired were Carmen and Rosa, who they decided would be their top girls, commanding a higher price than the others. This satisfied the two girls, who no longer held a grudge against either of them.

They also hired some local girls and quickly had a stable of half a dozen girls.

They passed the word to nearby towns that there was a "private" club in San Louisa, and were sure that the word would pass even further.

The first night they opened they got one customer, the town drunk, who thought they were serving liquor.

"Let's not get discouraged," Moran told Crystal. "It takes time to build up a clientele."

They were in the room they had both moved into in the converted rooming house. Since they were business partners, they figured Moran ought to move out of the hotel and move in with Crystal.

"Won't that look bad?" Crystal had asked beforehand. "I mean, you being the sheriff and all."

"I can do anything I want in this town, Crystal," Moran told her. "This is nothing like being a lawman in the States, where they spit on you if something goes wrong."

Now, sitting up in bed together, Crystal was noticeably upset, although she hadn't really said anything about it.

"I suppose you're right," she told him, leaning her head on his shoulder. "I just wanted this to be such a success."

"It will be."

A week later Crystal's was full, with men waiting downstairs for one of the girls to be free. It had become a popular stop for merchants and ranchers from the area, and word was spreading even further.

Moran had also hired three men—one from town, and two who were passing through and had agreed to stay on—as bouncers. They were all big, and they all wore guns and knew how to use them. There was very little trouble at Crystal's Palace with those men on duty. There was usually one man on duty inside, one off duty, and one making rounds on the street.

Moran had deputized all three, so that they were collecting pay from the Palace and from the town.

Crystal told her girls that they didn't have to do anything they didn't want to do. If a customer wanted something that they couldn't deliver, there was sure to be a girl in the building who could. Crystal's customers always went away satisfied—except, of course, when they asked for Crystal herself. Crystal was warming one bed these days—Moran's—and it wasn't for pay.

Well, not exactly, anyway. After all, she did still need some of his money until the Palace really starting making a profit.

As for the town, it was not making a profit from its new attraction at all, and contrary to what Red Moran might have thought, the town fathers didn't like it much. Starting with the mayor on down, they felt that the town should be getting something from the success of Crystal's Palace.

On the other hand, they were glad to have him and his money in town. He was still spending money in the town stores, even if he wasn't dropping any at the hotel.

So they wished that they were sharing in the profits of his cathouse, but were too afraid to ask. Afraid that he might leave town and take his money with him.

Also, he was doing a good job of upholding the law, and the mayor had asked him to keep the job permanently.

San Louisa was starting to look better and better to Moran as a place to settle down.

"We should give up."

Both Gilberto and Raquel heard the man say it.

Their three men were hunched around the campfire and one of them had just made that comment, talking about the search for Decker.

Gilberto came up behind the man, put his foot on his back and pushed. The man fell chest first into the campfire, yelled and rolled off of it, patting his chest with his hands.

"What—" he shouted.

"If you want to leave, then leave," Gilberto said, "but don't try to take the others with you."

"I was just giving my opinion, Gilberto," the man said. "We are spending a lot of time looking for this gringo. We are not making any money."

"Don't worry," Gilberto said, thinking about the price on the head of the man Decker was looking for, "there will be plenty of money for all of us—but if you want to leave . . ."

"I do not want to leave, Gilberto," the man said, earnestly.

"Then keep your opinions to yourself."

"*Si*, I will."

Gilberto and Raquel had their own campfire.

"You promised them some of our money?"

"I made no promises," Gilberto said. "I simply said that there would be enough money for all of us, and there will be—but they will not get any."

"We must find Decker before he finds this man,

Red Moran," Raquel pointed out to her brother, "or we will not get any of the money either."

"Do not worry," Gilberto said, "we will find him."

"Where do we go from here?" Raquel asked.

"When we were in the last town I heard about a place called San Louisa. Perhaps we can try there."

Raquel gave her brother an amused look.

"I also heard about this town. What you heard about San Louisa is that they have a new whorehouse there, with high-class girls. That is what you want to go there and see."

Gilberto shrugged.

"You must admit, it is as good a place as any to look next."

"Yes," Raquel said with a sigh, "I must admit that. How long will it take us to get there?"

"Three days."

"We had better get some sleep, then," she said. "We will have to start out early in the morning." She laid back on her blanket, then propped herself up on her elbows and asked, "How is your leg?"

"My leg is fine," he said tightly. "Go to sleep."

He ignored the leg as much as possible, even though it hurt much of the time. When he did think of it, it was only in terms of paying Decker back.

Gilberto put his head down on his saddle and thought about the money Decker was after.

First they would find him, then wait for him to find the man he was looking for. After that they would kill him, take the man and turn him in themselves for the reward.

Gilberto had no qualms about turning the man in. After he all, he *was* a gringo.

Chapter Twenty-six

Decker was starting to think he would never find Red Moran when he heard a story. It was about a man and a woman who opened a "private" whorehouse in a small town in the southern part of Mexico.

The woman was a beautiful red-haired American, and the man—also a gringo—had become sheriff of the town.

It takes a lot of money to set up a private operation like the one he was hearing about. He was two days' ride from the town of San Louisa, and decided to check it out.

Chapter
Twenty-seven

The mayor of San Louisa was presiding over a meeting of the town council. The five men seated at the table with him were all merchants in town. They were also frequent customers at the new Crystal's Palace.

"I say we must talk to the sheriff and his . . . his woman," the mayor was saying. "San Louisa should be prospering for being the site of their new and very successful business. Do any of you agree?"

The owner of the hotel agreed, because he was no longer getting any of Red Moran's money. In fact, Moran was getting his money when he went to the Palace.

The other four men, however—who owned the hardware store, the general store, the café and cantina, and the dress shop—were still getting their share of Moran's money.

Moran shopped at both the hardware and general stores, he and Crystal ate at the café and Crystal bought her dresses at the dress shop.

The mayor's proposal was being voted down, four to two.

The mayor decided to work on the owner of the café, Hector Dominguez.

"Hector, what will happen when señor Moran decides to put in a kitchen, or starts serving liquor? Where will you be then? Not only will you not be getting any of his money, but you'll be losing money."

Suddenly Hector decided to change his vote, but that still left the council at a three to three deadlock.

There was one member of the council who was not present, however, but the mayor didn't figure he could count of him for his vote.

The other member was Red Moran.

That night in bed Crystal passed on some information she had heard from the dress shop.

"Mrs. Mendez, the owner's wife, was telling one of the other women that there was a special meeting of the town council today."

"There was?" Moran asked. "I wasn't informed about that."

"That's because you—and I guess me—were the subjects of the meeting."

"Is that a fact?"

"Red, the town is getting tired of seeing us get rich and them not getting some of it. The mayor made a proposal that the council talk to us about it."

"And what was the council's vote?"

"Three to three."

"Deadlocked, so nothing will happen."

"Maybe not, and maybe the mayor will eventually get one more member to go his way."

"So what? Then they'll come and talk to us and we'll say no."

"And then what happens? You don't want to make enemies here, Red. We've got a good thing going and we don't want to mess it up."

"Stop worrying. We're not going to mess it up. What could they do? What could the mayor do. He's a silly little man who thinks he's really got some authority. He can't do anything to us."

"He could turn you in."

Moran looked at her and rubbed his jaw.

"That strutting peacock," Moran said, as if his feelings were hurt by the possibility. "When he needed a sheriff he came to me, and I've done a good job."

"That's when you were just sheriff, and you were spending your money around town. Now it's reversed. The merchants in town are spending their money here, and getting nothing back. The women in town are starting to complain."

"I've been thinking about serving liquor," Moran said, changing the subject. "While the customers are waiting, they could be spending money drinking."

"Boy, wouldn't the town fathers love that."

"Never mind what the town fathers want," Moran said, taking her into his arms. "They're all hypocrites, anyway. They spend as much time here as anyone."

He took Crystal into his arms and said, "Pretty

soon, baby, if we want, we'll be able to buy this town."

She grinned and said, "Would that make me a town mother?"

Chapter
Twenty-eight

When Decker rode into San Louisa he was surprised.

For a town with the hottest new whorehouse anywhere, it did not look very prosperous.

Decker passed by the whorehouse, and saw that other than the sign above the entrance, it looked much like any of the other buildings in town. He wondered what it looked like on the inside.

Later, when it opened, he'd find out.

As he turned his horse in at the livery he realized that he was starting to feel the anticipation he felt whenever he was closing in on his prey. He still had no concrete evidence that Moran was in town, but his instinct told him that he was.

And he had rarely gone wrong trusting his instincts.

As he had done in other towns when he was checking into the hotel, he looked through the register. He found what he was looking for three weeks back.

Red Moran had registered at the hotel.

"I hope you enjoy your stay, señor," the clerk said, handing him a key.

"I'm sure I will." He started for the steps and then turned back. "What time does Crystal's open?"

"Eight o'clock, señor."

"Thanks."

There were five hours before Crystal's Palace would open. Decker took the time to walk around town, enter some of the shops and get something to eat. Keeping his ears open, he found out several things.

First, Red Moran had managed to get himself appointed sheriff. Old habits die the hardest. He wondered if Moran had plans to rob the bank.

Secondly, many of the townspeople didn't like Moran, or the woman called Crystal. They resented the fact that they had opened a successful business and were not turning any of their profits over to the town.

Decker didn't know if he agreed with that. It certainly wouldn't make a man popular in town, but why should he turn any part of money he'd earned over to the town, unless it was willingly?

Still, the fact that Moran didn't seem to have many friends in town, and that he was sheriff, started Decker to thinking.

Moran was clean in Mexico, and Decker would have to take him all the way back to the Rio Grande at gunpoint before he could turn him in. If, as he suspected, Moran's situation in San Louisa was leading to where Decker thought it was leading, he'd soon make the same move here that he had made in all the other towns.

He'd try to rob the bank.

If Decker could catch him in the act, then he'd be able to turn him over to the law here in Mexico and let them provide transportation to the United States.

All he had to do was wait for the itch. And judging from the length of time Moran had been here, and his present situation, he should start feeling it just about now.

Chapter Twenty-nine

Try as he might Red Moran couldn't reach the itch. It seemed to be right at the center of his back where he couldn't reach it from any angle.

The Palace wasn't due to open for a couple of hours yet, and he was in the sitting room alone. He was looking for something to use to scratch it when he saw Gloria come in.

"Gloria," he called, "come here a minute."

Gloria was the newest girl in the stable. She had just come to Mexico from the United States. She was blonde and full-figured and she was the first girl Moran felt tempted to try himself. He hadn't been with another woman since he and Crystal had met, but that had been by choice. Now Gloria was here—younger than Crystal, and obviously eager—and the itch was starting.

"Yes, Red?" she asked. She had made no secret of the fact that she wouldn't mind warming the boss's bed.

"I've got an itch I can't reach," he said, realizing that the statement had two meanings—both of them correct.

"I'll be happy to help, Red."

"Right at the center of my back."

"A little to the right."

"Maybe if I put my hand under the shirt it would . . . feel better?"

"Maybe . . ."

She pulled his shirt out of his pants from behind and slid her hand beneath it. When she touched him it seemed to burn his skin. She ran her fingers across his broad back lovingly, and then used her nails to scratch him. As she did so she pushed her crotch up against his buttocks, and he could feel her heat right through their clothes.

"Oh, yeah, that's the spot," he said, closing his eyes as she scratched.

Suddenly, her hand was gone and he opened his eyes. Crystal was standing in the entrance to the room, glaring at both of them.

"I was just helping him reach an itch, Miss Crystal," the girl said.

"I'll bet you were, Gloria."

"I have to go upstairs now and . . . take care of something," Gloria said. She eased by Crystal carefully and left the room quickly.

"What was that all about?"

"She was telling the truth, Crys. I did have an itch that I couldn't reach."

"I'll bet. And little Gloria was the only one who could reach it, right?"

"Don't be ridiculous," he said. "If you had come in instead of her, you'd be scratching it."

"Don't bet on it!" she said frostily, her arms folded in front of her.

"Don't start acting like a wife, Crystal. We're not married."

"That's right, we're not; we're just partners."

Moran almost pointed out that it was his money that started the Palace, and that he could run it just as well without her, but he thought better of it.

"Look, honey—"

"Don't 'honey' me, Red," she said, turning around to leave the room, "just don't ever 'honey' me."

After she left he tucked his shirt back, realizing that he was experiencing more than just two kinds of itch.

Over the past couple of days he was realizing that he was getting the itch to move on. Once he had thought he would be able to settle down in San Louisa, but things had changed. Most of the townspeople disliked him, and he knew that the town council was starting to lean the mayor's way.

He was tired of being sheriff, tired of living here, and he was even getting tired of Crystal.

It was time to leave.

He figured he'd leave Crystal the Palace, and maybe even some money. She'd be able to make some more in no time. Just as he'd be able to run the place without her, she'd do fine without him.

And then there was the Bank of San Louisa.

Every day that he passed it he thought about going in and robbing it.

That was the biggest itch of all, and there wasn't anyone else—Gloria, Crystal—anyone, who could help him scratch it.

Chapter Thirty

That night when Decker entered Crystal's Palace, he was amazed at how the inside looked. He'd seen fancier places, but for a town like San Louisa, this was pretty fancy.

Already there were men waiting for a free girl, and he was also surprised to notice that there were no drinks being served. Perhaps that would be their next step.

He had not seen Red Moran on the streets of San Louisa the whole time he'd been there. Moran didn't seem to be taking his duties as sheriff all that seriously. He was sure, however, that he would be seeing the man here, tonight.

"Good evening, sir," a woman's voice said.

He turned his head and found himself looking into two of the greenest eyes he'd ever seen. The woman had pale skin and red hair, and a full, firm body fitted into a low-cut green dress. The cleft between her breasts was smooth and creamy.

"Welcome to Crystal's Palace," she said. "I am Crystal, your hostess."

"Thanks for the welcome."

"This is your first time here, isn't it?"

"Yes."

"Well, I should tell you that there is a membership fee before you can enter."

"How much?"

"Five dollars. After that you can pick out a girl and make your arrangements with her, depending on what you want."

"I don't see any girls," he said, looking around the sitting room, "only men."

"Well, all of our girls are busy at the moment. Would you like to stay?"

He took out five dollars and handed it to her.

"I'll stay."

"Thank you. I'm sure you won't regret it."

"Excuse me," he said as she turned to walk away.

"Yes?"

"If all of the girls are busy . . . what about the hostess?"

She smiled at him and said, "I'm afraid that would cost you more than you could afford."

"And it would probably be worth it, too."

Her smile broadened—and became more real—and she said, "You're very sweet. Please, have a seat and someone will be available shortly."

"Thanks."

Decker entered the sitting room, which was inhabited by cigar-smoking men who were engaged in conversation about various things. As he listened he heard some of them discussing business, and others discussing the merits of some of the girls who worked at the Palace. He counted almost a dozen men, and not all of them were Mexican, and not all of them were from his town.

He took a seat and lit up one of his own cigars, almost in self-defense. As he continued to look around the room he saw a couple of women come down the stairs, each of them Mexican and quite pretty. One was tall and full-breasted, while the other was shorter and slimmer. They each picked a man out who seemed to have been waiting for them and went back upstairs to work.

Decker was there almost a half an hour before he got what he wanted.

He was watching the steps from upstairs and recognized the man immediately.

He was tall, broad-shouldered, wearing a sheriff's star on his shirt, but what clinched it was the face. It was the same smooth, handsome face that was on the poster in his pocket.

There was twenty-five hundred dollars, coming down the stairs.

Behind him a stunning blonde woman came down, and at the foot of the stairs the redhead was glaring up at the two of them. From what Decker could see the fact that they were coming down at the same time was probably a coincidence, but the red-haired Crystal apparently didn't see it that way. She and Moran got into a heated discussion and Moran finally gave up and walked out.

Yep, Decker thought, things are sure heating up for Moran in this town. Shouldn't be long before he made his move.

The blonde eased past the redhead and came into the sitting room. She saw Decker just as he was standing up to leave and came walking over to him.

"Are you waiting for me, lover . . . I hope? I'm Gloria."

"Well, actually—" Decker said.

"He's waiting for me, Gloria," Crystal said, coming up behind the blonde.

Gloria turned and looked at Crystal in surprise.

"For you? But I thought—"

"This is by special request, dear," she said, looping her arm through Decker's. "Run along and take care of old Mr. Velasquez."

The blonde looked over at the white-haired, beer-bellied man Crystal was talking about, then rolled her eyes and walked over to him.

"He's the undertaker," Crystal said, "and he smells like it."

"Well, now that the joke is over," Decker said, disengaging her arm, "I think I'll be leaving."

"Leaving?" Crystal asked, looking puzzled. "But you did ask me if I was busy, didn't you?"

"Yes, but you said—"

"Well, I've changed my mind. I think you've been kept waiting so long that only the best will satisfy you." She put her arm through his again and said, "Shall we go upstairs?"

Decker recognized that this was a very dangerous situation. Crystal was obviously Moran's woman, and she was just doing this to get back at him after the argument they'd just had. At any moment, Moran could return and find them together.

Still, this was a place of business, and Decker really had nothing better to do with his time.

He looked at the creamy valley between her breasts again, and her green eyes, and said, "Yes, why don't we?"

Chapter Thirty-one

The next morning Decker slept late, because he'd had a strenuous time at Crystal's Palace the night before. Crystal had not been exaggerating her prowess in bed when she'd indicated that she was "the best."

He could also afford the luxury of sleeping late because now that he had successfully tracked his prey, and the man had no idea he was there, there was no need to rise early.

He had decided to give Moran until the end of the week—three days—to make his move. If nothing happened by then, he'd have to take the man by force and bring him back to the United States. From what he'd been able to gather, there wouldn't be any great hue and cry once Moran was gone. The man had apparently worn out his welcome here—even with his pretty partner.

Crystal awoke to an empty bed. That hadn't happened since she and Moran became partners, but she wasn't sorry.

Moran had obviously not come home last

night, but she found that she didn't mind. The man she had taken up to her room with her had more than made up for Moran's absence. In fact, he had made her realize that there was life after Moran.

She wondered how soon she'd be able to pay him back now that the business was going well. The original idea for the place *was* hers, and she really didn't need Moran anymore. After all, her original plan had been to simply use his money to set the Palace up. It had been ridiculous to start thinking that he might be the man for her.

There were many men out there, and it would be silly to tie herself down to one.

She rose and decided to take a hot bath. She had not yet been able to provide a private bath for herself, so she had been using the one downstairs, which was also used by the rest of the girls. It was a small price to pay, and soon enough she would have her own.

On the way down she thought that maybe if she could find out what Moran had done—why he was hiding out here in Mexico—she could turn him in herself. If what he had done had netted him so much money, there was sure to be some kind of a reward.

Moran had slept at the sheriff's office.

The argument the night before with Crystal had clinched it for him. All he had done was walk down the stairs, and because Gloria had been behind him Crystal had jumped to conclusions.

Well, Red Moran didn't need that kind of grief

from any woman, and he certainly didn't need the shit this town was heaping on him.

When he'd gotten to his office last night, he'd found the mayor waiting for him.

"What can I do for you, Mr. Mayor?"

"Sheriff—uh, this is very difficult for me to say."

"Well, just spit it out all at once, Mayor. That's usually the best way."

"The town council and I have, uh, reconsidered our position on your standing as sheriff."

"Is that a fact?"

"*Si*, we think that it would be better for everyone—especially the town—if we held an open election. Of course, you would be free to run . . ."

"So you'd like me to give you back my badge?"

"*Si*, if you, uh . . . would."

"Well, I won't."

"Señor, for the good of the town—"

"You and the council are upset about my extra business activities in town, Mayor. That is, you're mad because you're not getting as much of my money as you used to get. I was naive to think that you would have some other reason for welcoming me into your town, and for making me sheriff. Well, for better or for worse, I'm your sheriff."

"Señor," the mayor said, with more backbone than Moran would have given him credit for, "the town council can take your badge away from you."

"I happen to know that you and the council are

deadlocked on that question, Mayor—and I'm the tie-breaking vote. Guess which way I'd go."

Moran sat behind his desk at that point, laced his fingers behind his head and said, "Come back and see me when you get one more vote."

After that the mayor left, dragging his tail between his legs because his bluff had not worked . . .

Still, Moran decided, it was time to move on, and sometime in the next few days he'd make his move. First he had to decide just how much he wanted to leave Crystal. After all, the business had been started with his money.

And the other thing he had to do before he left was get that blonde, Gloria, into bed.

Gloria woke up and could still smell old Mr. Velasquez. She decided to go down and have a hot bath before sitting down to take stock and formulate her plans.

She had been in Mexico long enough.

Gilberto and Raquel gave their horses to one of the men and went into the cantina. It did not serve liquor that early, but they were more interested in food than liquor.

They had camped an hour outside of town last night because they wanted time to look the town over. To this end they had sent in one of their men—Juan—to look around. He had returned late with the news that the town had one sheriff, and apparently no deputies, and the sheriff was rarely seen on the street. At first light they had mounted up and ridden in, and now they'd have breakfast sitting at a real table rather than around a fire.

From where they had camped they had easily picked out the whorehouse. It was the building that was most lit, and had the most traffic in and out.

"I am surprised you were able to contain yourself last night," Raquel said after they had ordered breakfast.

"What do you mean?"

"I thought you would run right down to that whorehouse the first chance you saw."

"My sister, I am not controlled by animal lust. Besides, tonight will be soon enough."

"First we must find out if Decker has been here, or is still here—and if he is here we must not be seen."

"He will recognize either of us, but perhaps not the others."

"We will see, Gilberto."

When Gloria reached the bathroom she found that Crystal was already there, sitting in one of the two tubs.

"Oh, sorry," she said, starting to back out.

"There's another tub, Gloria," Crystal said. "You can come in and use it."

"I wouldn't want to intrude—"

"It's no intrusion, really."

Gloria came in, wondering what Crystal had on her mind that she was being so accommodating.

Gloria heated her own water, filled the tub, and

then took off her robe. She was aware of Crystal's appraising look as she stepped into the tub.

"You have a lovely body, you know," Crystal said.

Uncomfortable with the compliment from another woman, Gloria simply said, "Thank you."

"You're not like most of the whores here, Gloria."

"What do you mean?"

"Carmen, Rosa and the others, they're all doing this because there's nothing else they can do. You, on the other hand, are a lot smarter that they are."

Gloria smiled thinly.

"That's not really saying that much, Miss Crystal."

Crystal threw her head back and laughed.

"Don't I know it. You know, you and I are the only non-Mexicans here. Maybe we could become friends."

Gloria doubted that, but said, "I think I would like that."

"There's something you should know about me and Red Moran, then."

"I know he's your man, and I wouldn't—"

"That's just it," Crystal said. "He's my partner, Gloria, but he's not my man. If you want him, you're welcome to him."

Gloria frowned.

"You're from Texas, aren't you?" Crystal continued.

"Yes."

"Did you ever hear of Moran there?"

So that's what she was after. She was trying to find out Moran's background.

"No," Gloria lied, "I never heard of him until I reached here. Why?"

"Oh, no reason," Crystal said, soaping herself, "no reason at all . . ."

Chapter Thirty-two

Decker woke and walked to the window. He opened it and took a deep breath. *This*, he thought, *smells like a town*, and he found he missed the fresh smell of the Rio del Gato.

Staring out the window he saw three men walking from the hotel to the cantina, as if they had just checked in and were now on their way to get a drink. He almost thought nothing of it when he frowned and took a second look.

If he was not mistaken, those were the same three men he and Jose had knocked unconscious in the livery—Gilberto Diaz's men. Had he seen any of them alone he would not have recognized them, but all three together were hard to miss.

So, in addition to having Moran in town, he also had those three. Could Gilberto and Raquel be far behind?

It wasn't that big of a surprise that they had been able to escape from Jose. After all, he wasn't exactly the model of an efficient lawman. The question this brought up, however, was whether or not their presence here in San Louisa was a co-incidence.

He thought not.

How they had found him he did not know, but the fact that they had bothered could only have been fuelled by a desire for revenge.

Things were about to get much more compli-cated than he needed.

Chapter Thirty-three

Before meeting Gilberto and Raquel at the cantina, Juan, Martinez and Orlando went to the hotel to secure three rooms. Gilberto and Raquel would each have their own, while the three men would be forced to share one.

While waiting for their rooms, Juan went through the register and saw Decker's name. This was the news he gave the bandit leader and his sister, now.

"Then he is here," Gilberto said.

"How much further will we have to follow him to find the man he seeks?" Raquel asked. She looked at Juan and asked, "When did he arrive?"

"Yesterday."

She looked at her brother.

"If he is not leaving today, then he has found the man he is hunting for."

"Here, in this town?"

"Yes."

"Then we have them both."

"All we must do is identify the man," Raquel said, "and then we will no longer need Decker."

"Identifying the man should not be difficult," Gilberto said. "He will also be a gringo, and there are not many here."

"The sheriff," Juan said.

"What?" Gilberto asked.

"The sheriff is a gringo."

Gilberto and Raquel exchanged glances.

"The three of you move about the town and find out what you can about the sheriff. What his name is, when he came to town, when he became sheriff and anything else that you can," Raquel instructed. "You will find us at the livery stable." They looked to Gilberto for confirmation, but she snapped, "Go!" and they moved.

"Why the livery stable?" Gilberto asked his sister. He had been looking forward to sleeping in a real bed.

"Gilberto, we will have to stay out of sight so that Decker does not see us."

"If he is staying at the hotel—"

"Yes. We will have to stay somewhere else."

"There is nowhere else."

"Then we will camp outside of town," Raquel said. "If he sees us it will ruin everything. I don't want him to see us until the last moment of this life."

"And it will be my pleasure to kill him," Gilberto said.

"And mine to watch."

When Moran left his office he saw the three men leaving the cantina. They were strangers, and Moran had been a lawman long enough—and enough times—to distrust strangers. He watched their progress as they crossed the street and then suddenly split up.

He decided to follow one of them and see where he would lead.

His instinct was more one of self-preservation than anything else. The phrase "bounty hunter" had only recently been brought up, and now there were three strangers in town. True, they were Mexicans, but Mexicans could collect a bounty just as well as gringos.

With the direction his thoughts were taking this morning, it definitely was time to start moving again.

San Louisa had now lost *all* of its charms.

Chapter Thirty-four

When Decker left his hotel he saw Moran leaving his office. Ducking back into the lobby he watched and saw Moran watching the three bandits. When the three men separated, Moran started to follow one of them.

Was the man acting like a real sheriff all of a sudden? That wasn't very likely. He was probably acting out of a natural distrust of strangers, and that made Decker happy that Moran had not seen him yet. As lawmen went, Moran had not exactly been very visible yesterday.

Decker decided to tail Moran, because if the man was that jumpy, this might be the day he'd make his move.

For the next hour he followed Moran as "The Lawman" followed the bandit. The bandit, on the other hand, seemed to simply be roaming the streets, stopping occasionally in a store to speak with the merchants.

It was odd behavior for a bandit.

While following the two men Decker kept an eye out for Gilberto or Raquel, but they were more than likely keeping a low profile so as not to run into him.

Decker knew he was going to have to do something about them well before he made a move on Moran. The only problem with that was that there were five of them, and only one of him.

Unless, of course . . . and the answer came with a jolt of irony . . . unless the town lawman could be persuaded to back him.

Moran didn't know him. What if he became convinced that Gilberto, Raquel and their men were bounty hunters?

It was a big 'what if?', but if it worked . . .

After the initial hour Moran gave up on tailing the bandit, and crossed the street to go in the opposite direction. Decker stepped into a doorway and watched the sheriff to see where he was headed. When it was safe to do so he stepped out and followed him.

Moran eventually went into a café—hopefully for breakfast—and by then Decker's plan was completely formed in his mind.

He entered the café, found Moran, and went over to sit with him.

Chapter Thirty-five

"Can I help you?" Moran asked. He was frowning. He disliked the idea that there was another stranger in town, and that the man had suddenly appeared at his table.

A waiter came over and Decker said, "Coffee for two, and bring the sheriff whatever he wants for breakfast."

Moran, his appetite possibly ruined, said, "Just the coffee."

"Nothing more? That's not the right way to start a day, Sheriff."

"Why don't we start it with an explanation from you, friend?"

"Well, I saw you come in here and figured maybe you'd like another gringo to talk to. You know, about home and all that?"

"You were wrong."

"All right, then *I* wanted somebody to talk to."

"About what?"

"About this little problem I'm having."

"Which is?"

"Well, this is a little embarrassing to admit," Decker said, scratching his head, "but the fact is I'm a wanted man back in the States."

"Is that a fact?"

"Yep. A thousand dollars."

"That's quite a price."

"My problem is that there are some people in town who are looking to collect."

At that Moran suddenly looked interested. They suspended the conversation while the waiter put down a pot of coffee and two cups.

"Something else?" he asked.

"No!" Moran said firmly. After the waiter had left he looked at Decker and said, "Bounty hunters?"

Decker nodded, and spread the fingers of his hand to show Moran. "Five of them."

"Five? On a thousand-dollar bounty? That's only two hundred apiece."

"Two hundred dollars is a lot of money to some people—but I don't think all five will collect."

"What do you mean?"

"Well, the leaders of this particular group are a brother and sister, and I know them. Their name is Diaz. He's as ugly as sin, but she's beautiful—and deadly. Anyway, I think they picked up these three other men to help them because they knew I'd recognize them. They're either going to pay these fellas about fifty dollars each, or . . ."

"Or what?"

"Or they will kill them when the job is done. After I'm dead, I mean."

Moran thought it over.

"That would make sense. That way it would be a straight two-way split, with no expenses."

"I need your help."

"Why don't you just ride out?"

"They'd just follow me and I'd have to face them somewhere else down the road. At least here I've got a fellow countryman to help me out. You will help me, won't you, Sheriff? I mean, I'm not trying to wave the flag in your face or anything, but us gringos have to stick together."

"You've got a lot of nerve asking me to help you. I'm the law and you're a wanted man."

"Not in Mexico."

"What's your name?"

Decker picked the name he'd seen on another poster of a man he knew was still on the loose.

"Mike Sideman. If you got any posters in your office you can look it up."

"I don't get posters from the United States down here."

"Well then, you'll have to take my word for it, Sheriff. "I mean, why would I tell you I was wanted if I wasn't?"

Moran nodded, sipped his coffee, and then said, "All right."

"All right . . . what?"

"I'll help you."

"I knew I could count on you!"

"Are you staying at the hotel?"

"Yeah."

"Go back to your room and wait for me. I'll find these people and check them out."

"I really appreciate this, Sheriff," Decker said, standing up.

"Forget it. What name are you using?"

Decker hesitated just a second. He was registered under his own name, and if Moran recognized it, his disguise would be revealed.

"Decker."

No flicker of recognition, and Decker was looking very closely.

"Okay, Decker. Back to your hotel and wait to hear from me."

"Thanks, Sheriff."

Moran signalled to the waiter and dismissed Decker. "Get out and let me eat my breakfast."

Decker left and walked back to the hotel. This might go off better than he planned. If Moran found Gilberto and Raquel and tossed them in jail, the other three men would be left to wander aimlessly about town. Without the brother and sister to tell them what to do, they'd be lost.

And the Diaz siblings would be out of Decker's way.

Chapter Thirty-six

Moran ate his breakfast thoughtfully, virtually without tasting it, and thought about what the man called Decker had just told him.

Decker had to be telling the truth. Why would a man tell a lawman he was wanted if he wasn't?

That meant that Moran was right in following the stranger earlier. He was one of the three men that the two bounty hunters had working for them.

If they were here tracking Decker for a thousand dollars, wouldn't they be aware of the price on Moran's head? The last he had seen, the price was fifteen hundred. It might have been increased after that Pemberton job, because that had been the first job where he'd used violence.

So, if they were here looking for Decker and spotted Moran, would they recognize him?

Moran was going to have to do something before that situation presented itself.

He finished his breakfast and left the cantina looking for the two bounty hunters: an ugly man and a beautiful woman.

They shouldn't prove too hard to find.

Gilberto and Raquel were in the livery stable, waiting for their men to report.

"This is not what I had in mind when we came to town," Gilberto said, lying back on a bed of hay. Raquel was sitting next to him, her arms behind her, propping her up.

"Neither did I, but we cannot afford to have Decker see us. You can visit your whorehouse tonight, my brother."

"I look forward to it. And what will you do tonight?"

"Stay out of sight. My appetites are not as uncontrollable as yours."

"Your appetites are just as strong as mine, little sister," Gilberto said, running his finger up his sister's right arm.

"Then perhaps it is simply that I am stronger than you, Gilberto. I control my urges rather than letting them control me."

"Like you did with that sheriff? Tell me, did you kill him before, or after?"

"None of your business."

Gilberto laughed, and stopped when he heard someone enter the livery.

"It is probably them," Raquel said.

They both stood up, preparing to step out of the stall they were sitting in, when a man barred their way. He was holding a gun in his hand, and when he saw them he cocked it.

"Hello, bounty hunters."

Moran checked around town and found out that the three strangers had been asking questions about him. Though he wasn't much liked in town anymore, the merchants freely gave him this information because they liked strangers even less.

Moran checked around further and found out that a man and woman fitting the description he had were seen walking over to the livery.

He went to the livery and entered cautiously, gun drawn. He heard two voices—male and female— from a stall in the back, and walked lightly to it.

In the stall, just getting to their feet, were the man and woman he was looking for.

God, but the woman was beautiful! If he had her in his stable at the Palace he'd consider staying on, because she would be a gold mine.

Right now, however, she was a threat.

"Hello, bounty hunters," he said, cocking the hammer on his gun.

They froze, and frowned at him. The look on the man's ugly face was particularly comical.

"What did you call us, señor?"

"You heard me—and keep your hands away from your guns. Using you left hand now, take them out and toss them out of the stall."

"*Jefe*, you are making a big error here," Gilberto said, doing as he was told. Raquel also obeyed.

"Okay, one at a time, step out of the stall. Hey!"

he snapped at Gilberto when he took a step forward. "Ladies first, pig!"

Gilberto threw a hard look at the lawman, but stepped back.

"A gentleman," Raquel said, "and a handsome one, too. Could we not work something out, *Jefe*?"

"You mean like a roll in this here hay?" Moran asked.

Raquel shrugged.

"That could be arranged."

"We might be getting around to that later, lady, but right now you and your brother come with me. Come on, ugly. Your turn. Step out."

"How did you know we were brother and sister?" Raquel asked, puzzled.

"A little bird told me. All right, let's move. We're going to jail."

"A little bird named Decker?" Raquel asked.

"You're a smart lady."

"And you are not very smart, señor," Raquel said. "It is Decker who is the bounty hunter."

"Right, and he's chasing the five of you, right?"

"Even if we are bounty hunters," Gilberto broke in, to Raquel's annoyance, "why are you taking us to jail?"

"Haven't you heard? Sheriffs don't like bounty hunters, or haven't you been at it long enough to know that?"

"Sheriff, I assure you," Raquel said, "Decker is the bounty hunter."

"Well, if he is, and he's tracking you, that means you're wanted, so you'll feel right at home in my jail."

"Decker is here looking for someone else."

"And why are you here?"

"Looking for Decker."

"But you're not bounty hunters."

"That is right."

"Hey, this is making more sense by the minute, lady." By now they had reached the sheriff's office. "All right, inside. I wish I could offer you a choice of cells, but I only have one."

He pushed Gilberto into it, and then said to Raquel, "If you please?"

Exasperated, Raquel stepped into the cell. Moran locked it and put the key in his desk.

"Now, if you're real nice I'll send you something to eat later."

"Sheriff—" Raquel shouted, but the man had already gone.

"What is going on?" Gilberto demanded aloud.

"Decker has outsmarted us," Raquel said. "He has told the sheriff a story, and since his story came first, the sheriff will continue to believe him."

"Juan and the others will get us out," Gilberto said.

"Juan and the others cannot find their pants unless we set them on fire. We will have to think of something, my brother, and fast."

Chapter Thirty-seven

It had worked!

Decker watched from his window as Moran marched Gilberto and Raquel to jail.

With those two out of the way, his job would be a lot simpler.

Watching closely he could see that both Raquel and her brother were talking to the lawman. Obviously, they were trying to tell him that he was making a mistake. Just as obviously, Moran was not buying it. How could they convince the sheriff that they were not hunting Decker for a bounty? He certainly wouldn't believe that Decker—one man alone—would be hunting for five.

When the knock came at his door Decker knew it was Moran because he had seen the man cross the street to the hotel.

When he opend the door Moran stuck his gun in his face and cocked the hammer.

"What's going on, Sheriff?" he asked, backing into the room.

"Just being cautious, Decker. I'll take your gun—left hand, please."

"What do you mean, cautious?"

"Well, I only have your word that those two are bounty hunters, and they claim that you are. Either way, I don't like bounty hunters, so I'll just lock you up too until I can satisfy myself about who is who."

This was not the way the plan was supposed to work, Decker thought.

"You're going to put me in a cell with them?"

"Now, I wouldn't do that to a fellow gringo, Decker. There's a woodshed out behind the sheriff's office. I'm going to lock you in there. Let's go."

"You're making a mistake, Sheriff, really."

"Sure, Decker, sure. Let's take a walk."

When the door closed on Decker he found himself in total darkness. Even the cell with Gilberto and Raquel might have been better than this.

It was definitely time for a new plan.

He sat down with his back against one wall of the shed and surveyed his own private cell. As his eyes began to get accustomed to the dark he could see that there was some light coming from some cracks between the wood, but by pressing with both hands he determined that whoever had build this shed had done a fine job.

It was strong enough to hold a horse.

He looked around the floor and saw a few pieces of wood, but the shed had apparently not been used for some time. The ground beneath him was damp, and he knew that his butt would get cold and numb soon enough.

He still had his matches and cigars, so he lit one up and used the match to take a better look at things. All around the floor there were small chunks of wood that he might be able to use to make a small fire. At least he'd have some light and some heat.

He gathered the pieces of wood together, but they were a little damp and would not light immediately. He checked pockets and found the poster on Moran. He couldn't burn that, he needed it. Checking further he found an old poster in his back pocket that he didn't need anymore.

Using the paper he started a fire, and eventually the wood pieces caught. It wouldn't last very long and maybe he should have saved them for later, when it got dark out and cooler, but he didn't intend to still be in that shed when it got dark.

The only question was, how to get out?

He settled down by the fire to think that one over.

His gun was gone, but he still had his gunbelt. That meant he still had his cartridges. He could pry some of them open and use the gunpowder inside. Could he blow the door that way? Probably not. Enough powder to do that would probably kill him, or at least deafen him. Besides which, he probably didn't have enough powder to do the job.

Briefly, he considered setting one of the walls on fire, but discarded that. The entire structure would catch fire fairly quickly, and he'd be barbecued before the fire weakened one of the walls enough for him to break through.

He spent some time kicking at the door and the

walls, looking for a weak point and finding none. He also thought that someone might hear the noise and let him out, but that wasn't the case, either.

The fire flickered and he looked around for more wood chips to burn. He cleaned the floor of the shed, and was quickly left with nothing but hard-packed dirt.

Wait a minute.

Dirt?

The entire floor of the shed was dirt. Whoever had built it had not bothered to build a wooden floor. Even if they had, he might have been able to pry up a floorboard and get at the dirt. The whole point being that dirt can be dug up.

Using his hands he tried to start a hole, but succeeded only in breaking two fingernails. He could have used a large piece of wood to dig with, but all of the wood he'd found on the floor was now in the fire—and none of it had been large enough to use as a shovel.

If only he had a shovel.

His hands went to his belt buckle as if of their own volition. It was fairly large, and it was metal. Quickly he removed his gunbelt, then took off his belt and looked at the belt buckle. The edges were fairly sharp, but would they last long enough to dig a hole in the hard-packed dirt of the floor so that he could slide under one of the walls?

He'd never know until he tried.

Chapter Thirty-eight

"I think I have an idea," Raquel said.

"What?"

"The man Decker is looking for. What if it is the sheriff?"

"The sheriff a wanted man?"

"Not in our country, but in theirs."

"And the man comes down here to hide out and becomes sheriff?"

"Can you think of a better irony?"

"If that is true then we must find out."

"It is logical, my brother. The sheriff is the only other gringo that we have seen in town, and Decker is in no hurry to leave. That just might be the answer! So we must convince him that Decker is hunting him, and that we can help him get Decker."

"How do we do that?"

"Leave that to me, brother," Raquel said. "When it comes to men, I can be very convincing."

"Yes, I noticed that from the wonderful job you did of keeping us out of jail."

She gave her brother a withering look and

turned away. Now all they had to do was hope the sheriff came back sometime in the near future.

Moran felt better with all three of them locked up. He wasn't too worried about the other three men. They were sure to be hirelings, incapable of thinking for themselves. As long as they didn't know where to find their bosses, they'd be no problem.

Moran thought about Decker and frowned. The coincidence of too many strangers hitting town at the same time bothered him. It was too much to accept. He decided that there was no time to leave town like the present.

Not right this minute, but certainly today, even if it was after dark.

First, he had to wrap up his business.

With the Palace closed and the girls out shopping, Gloria figured it was time to make her move. Crystal was in her office—the office she shared with Moran—and she was alone. Gloria took out her derringer and garter holster, slipped it on, and then let herself out of her room.

Crystal sat at her desk, sulking. There was no way she could cut Moran out. They just hadn't been open long enough to make that kind of money. There had to be another way to convince Moran to leave without him wanting a piece of the business.

When the knock came at her door she thought it was one of the girls coming to her with a problem.

That was what she was there for, she had told them. Her door was always open to them.

She was going to have to get rid of the bitch.

When she opened the door she was surprised to see that it was Gloria.

"May I come in?"

"Is there something I can do for you?" Crystal asked.

"Yes, if I could have a moment of your time."

"All right, come in."

Crystal closed the door and turned to face Gloria, who had swiftly removed her derringer from its holster.

"What's this?" Crystal demanded.

"You're going back with me, Crystal."

"Back where?"

"To Texas."

"No!"

"Yes, you are. You have some unpaid debts there."

"And you're the bill collector?"

"That's right," Gloria said. "I'm the collector."

The door opened then and Moran stepped in.

"Red, she's got a gun."

"I can see that."

"Well, do something!"

He did. Smiling, he put his hands in the air.

Chapter Thirty-nine

Decker was pleasantly surprised to find that after he had broken through the hard surface, the dirt beneath was loose and easy to dislodge. The belt buckle worked perfectly as a shovel and though it was hard work he soon saw daylight shining through the hole. All he had to do was widen it a bit, and he'd be able to slide out beneath the wall.

Anxious to be out he finally discarded the belt buckle and used both hands to scoop out large portions of dirt. When he had it large enough he pushed his belt and gunbelt through, and then followed.

He had a moment of panic when he got stuck, but by wiggling he managed to dislodge enough dirt to loosen himself, and then he was out.

He squinted at the sunlight, and while his eyes adjusted to it he slipped his belt back on, and then his gunbelt.

Standing up he decided that first he needed a gun, and then he needed to find Moran.

It was time to stop playing around and get the business at hand finished.

He went back to his hotel, and the clerk stared at his dirty, sweaty clothes. He went up to his room and pulled his spare gun out of his saddlebags, a heavy Navy Colt that he had taken from a sailor on San Francisco's Barbary Coast some years ago. He slid it into the front of his belt and left to find Moran.

He went first to the sheriff's office, entered cautiously and quickly determined that Moran was not there.

However, Gilberto and Raquel were.

"Well, Raquel. *Como esta?*"

"Hijo de cabron!" she spat at him.

"Oh, I don't know what that means, but it doesn't sound good."

"I am going to kill you, Decker."

"Gilberto, that's not something you say to an armed man from behind bars." Decker took the Navy Colt from his belt, pointed it at Gilberto and cocked the hammer. The man tried to find somewhere to hide in the small cell without success.

"If I thought there was a chance of you carrying out your threat, I'd kill you right here."

"You can't!" Gilberto said, covering his head with his arms.

"Oh, leave him alone, Decker," Raquel said. "What do you want?"

"Nothing, from you. I was looking for Moran." When she looked puzzled, he said, "The sheriff."

"Then he is the man you are hunting for."

"Is that why you followed me?" Decker asked. "For the reward on the man *I* was following?"

"Why else?"

"And I thought you liked me, and missed me."

"If you let me out of here I will not miss you," she threatened.

"Now you're starting to sound like your brother. Oh well," he said, easing the hammer down on the Colt and tucking it into his belt, "I have business to attend to."

"Decker!" she shouted as he started for the door.

"Yes?"

"Decker," she said again, her tone lower, sexier, "you can let me out and leave Gilberto here. You were right. I do miss you. We never had a chance to . . . get to know each other."

"You know, you're a dangerous woman, Raquel," he said, walking back towards the cell.

She *was* beautiful, all wild hair and eyes, proud breasts and long legs.

"I'm almost tempted to let you out."

"It can be wonderful, Decker," she whispered. "It can be unbelievable."

"I know," Decker said sadly. "I know it could."

He started away again and she called out again.

"Decker!"

"What?"

"You look like you've been rolling in . . . how do you say it?"

"Shit?"

"*Si*, that is it. Shit."

"Don't worry, with the money I get for Moran, I can buy a whole new wardrobe. *Adios*, baby."

"Decker!"

The next place to look, he thought, was Crystal's Palace.

Chapter Forty

When he got to the building he found the front door locked. Knocking on it would only alert Moran, if he was inside. Decker went around to the back, checking windows, and finally found the one he was looking for. He was surprised by what he saw through it.

Moran was there with his hands in the air, his gun still holstered. Decker could see his own gun, too, tucked into Moran's belt. Crystal was there, and the blonde whore from the night before was holding a derringer on both of them.

What the hell was going on now?

He listened intently at the window.

"That's a very tiny gun, Gloria," Moran said.

"Don't worry, it makes very deadly holes."

"I'm sure it does. You ladies want to tell me what this is about? Surely you're not fighting over me."

"Ha!" Crystal said.

"I'm taking Crystal back to Texas, Red."

"Why?"

"She stole some money from my father, made him the laughingstock of town. People are talking behind his back about how the old fool fell for a younger woman and got what he deserved."

"I'm sorry," Crystal said. "I really liked your father, Gloria, but I needed the money."

"Sure, everybody needs money. When I got back to town and heard what had happened, I got your description and started tracking you and finally found you here. I was lucky that you're a redhead. There aren't that many in Mexico, and you made an impression wherever you went."

"But I left Texas over three months ago."

"And I've been tracking you that long. We're going back, Crystal."

"You can't take me away from here. I'm not wanted here in Mexico."

"You are in Texas, and when I get you over the border I'll turn you in."

"Is there a reward?" Moran asked.

"No," Gloria said. "She broke the law, but nobody bothered to put out a poster on her. After all, all she did was remove an old fool from his money. When I get her back, though, I'll make sure she's prosecuted."

"Well, baby," Moran said to Crystal, "I guess this is goodbye."

"You bastard!" Crystal shouted at him. "You could stop her!"

"She might shoot me."

"You want her to take me back so you can have this place to yourself."

"Actually, I was planning on leaving today

anyway, Crystal, but now a couple of things have come up that might change my mind."

With Crystal gone he wouldn't have to split the profits with anyone, and if he could convince the woman in the jail cell to work for him, his profits might even double. Of course, he might have to make certain concessions to the town council, and he knew he'd eventually get bored again, but for now things were once again taking an interesting turn.

"She's all yours, Gloria—is that your name, by the way? Gloria?"

"My name is Anne Merritt."

"Well, Anne Merritt, in one respect I'm sorry you're leaving. I was planning on getting to know you a whole lot better."

"You don't understand, Red," Gloria—or Anne Merritt—said.

"What don't I understand, Anne?"

"You're coming back with us."

"I'm going back?" he asked, laughing. "Now, why would I want to go back?"

"Because there's a poster out on you, and I aim to collect the twenty-five hundred dollar reward."

"Twenty-five hundred—now how would you know about that?"

"It's my business to know, Red," Anne said. "I'm a bounty hunter."

Moran stared at her, said, "Jesus!" and Crystal started to laugh.

Decker thought it was funny, too. He'd travelled all this way and put all this time into tracking

Moran, and the man had been snatched out from under his nose by a woman!

His humor faded quickly, though, as Decker realized the dangerous position Anne Merritt had put herself in. She was in a small room with two people who didn't want to go with her, and all she was armed with was a derringer.

There was a back door to the office, and Decker moved towards it, hoping that the blonde woman would ask Moran for his guns.

"All right, Moran, I'll take your guns," Anne Merritt said.

"My guns? So you can use them against me instead of that toy?"

"I assure you I'm quite profficient with this toy, Moran. Your guns, please."

"Sure, honey, here."

With that Moran took Decker's gun from his belt and tossed it to the woman. Surprised, she made a move to catch it, and Moran took advantage of the moment. He took two quick steps and pushed Crystal into Anne Merritt. The derringer in Anne's hand went off and Crystal cried out. She fell to the floor, clutching her stomach. Anne looked at Moran and saw that he had his gun pointed at her. She had not caught the other gun, and her derringer was pointing at the floor.

"Drop it," Moran said.

She obeyed.

"She needs a doctor," Anne said, squatting down by Crystal.

"A doctor can't help her. She's gut-shot."

Anne looked at the wound and saw that it was off to the right.

"She's not," she insisted. "A doctor can help her."

"Get her one when I'm gone, then."

Moran moved around behind the desk, opened a drawer and took out a sheaf of money. Seeing Anne watching him he smiled at her.

"We haven't had time to put in a safe yet," he said, tucking the money inside his shirt.

"Bastard!" Crystal said from the floor, her pain evident in her voice.

"It was nice while it lasted, ladies," Moran said. He started for the office door, then stopped and turned back to them.

"Listen, Gloria—I mean, Anne. If I leave you here you're not gonna try and track me down, are you?"

"You damn well better believe I am, Moran!"

Moran shook his head and said, "That's too bad. You're so pretty."

He pointed his gun at her.

Chapter Forty-one

Outside Decker turned the knob of the back door slowly and found it locked. He moved back to the window and heard the shot. He saw Crystal fall and watched Moran move around behind the desk and take out some money.

He wasn't going to leave the two women alive. He couldn't, especially since the blonde had turned out to be a bounty hunter.

He hurried back to the door, Colt in hand, braced himself, and then kicked out at the door as hard as he could just above the doorknob.

As the door slammed open Moran turned and brought his gun to bear on it. Anne Merritt took the opportunity to leap from her crouch, banging into him and knocking him off balance.

Decker entered in a crouch and saw Moran staggering for his balance.

"Moran!" he shouted.

Moran braced himself against the wall with one hand and pointed his gun.

"Don't!" Decker shouted, and fired.

His bullet struck Moran high on the right shoulder. Moran squeezed the trigger of his gun but his shot went wild as he was spun around to face the wall. He stuck there for a moment, then slid down the wall to the floor.

Anne Merritt hurried to him and pulled the gun free from his nerveless fingers.

"Are you all right?" Decker asked Anne.

"I'm fine, but they both need a doctor."

Decker checked Crystal's wound, then went over and looked at Moran's. It was his opinion that they would both live.

"We'll get them one."

"Decker!" Moran said. His eyes were glazed, but he recognized Decker.

"That's me."

"You're the . . . bounty hunter," Moran said through clenched teeth.

"One of them, anyway," Decker said, looking at Anne Merritt.

"Why . . . such a high price . . . for a few banks?" Moran asked.

"Because that bank manager you hit in Pemberton died, Moran. You're wanted for murder."

Moran closed his eyes.

Anne Merritt said to Decker, "Where'd you come from?"

"I just happened along."

"I'm glad you did."

"Me too."

She looked him up and down and then said, "You could have dressed better, though."

"Didn't have time to change. Why don't you go

for the doctor while I wait with them," he said. "Crystal's in no condition to be moved."

"All right. I'll be right back."

She moved to the back door and started out, but as she did there was a shot and a bullet dug into the door frame just above her head.

"What the—" Decker said.

From behind him he heard a low laugh, like a death rattle, and turned to look at Moran.

"My boys, Decker," Moran said, gritting his teeth against the pain. "Now you've got to face my boys. You ain't taking me nowhere!"

Chapter Forty-two

Anne Merritt fell into a crouch, Moran's gun in her right hand. She peered outside and pulled her head back in when there was another shot.

"How many of them?" Decker asked.

"I can't tell," Anne said, "but he's got three men."

"Cover him," Decker said. Anne turned and pointed her gun at Moran as Decker moved to the door. He chanced a look outside, and a bullet stuck the doorjamb, spraying his face with wood splinters.

"Can't see how many of them there are," he said, "but we'll have to assume that all three are out there."

"How did they know—"

"Who knows? One of them might have seen me in the back and went to get the others. When they heard the shots it wouldn't be hard to figure out that something was wrong."

"Maybe if we tell them who we are and that we're taking Moran back—"

"We're not lawmen, Anne—and Moran is the

man who pays them. They're not going to let us take him."

"So what do we do?" she asked. "We're pinned down and we don't even have a sheriff to turn to."

"We'll just have to get out of this ourselves," he said. He pointed to the office door and asked, "Where does that lead to?"

"The sitting room."

"All right. Keep him covered and keep this door closed." He slammed the door closed, and it was immediately peppered with bullets.

"Where are you going?"

"Through the building to the front. Maybe I can get out that way and get behind them."

"Be careful," she said. "You're outnumbered three to one."

"Don't remind me."

He started for the door, then stopped when Crystal moaned. He leaned over and saw that she was semiconscious. He face was covered with sweat, and her complexion was waxy and pale.

"How is she?"

"She's in shock. If we don't get her out of here fast she'll die."

Anne turned to Moran and said, "If you ever had any real feelings about Crystal you'll let us get her out of here to a doctor!"

"Sorry, sweetie," Moran said, "but I've got more important things to worry about than her life."

"Yeah," Decker said, "his neck. If he tries anything, Anne, kill him. He pays off dead or alive."

"Right."

Decker went through the door to the sitting

room and closed it behind him. He was in the dark and he waited for his eyes to adjust. When they did he was able to see his way to the front door. He moved across the room with his gun ready and made it to the door with no problems. All three of Moran's men must have been outside. Luckily, they hadn't thought of getting to the office through here.

When he reached the front door he peered out the window next to it to the street. He couldn't see anyone, but then they would be taking cover near the side of the house so they could look down the alleyway. As quietly as he could he unlocked the door, opened it and stepped out onto the front porch. He closed the door and fell into a crouch.

He remained quiet that way for a few moments and was finally rewarded when he heard voices. He couldn't make out what they were saying, but they were male voices, and had to be Moran's men.

The way Decker figured it, these fellas were working strictly for money, and there was no loyalty involved here. Crystal's Palace hadn't been set up long enough for loyalty to have become a factor.

He moved in a crouch to the end of the porch, and from there he was able to see two men, one on either side of the mouth of the alley. There was more than half a moon, and plenty of light to see by. From where they were, looking down the dark alley, anyone who stepped into the open doorway would be a perfect target.

There were two ways he could have played this. He could simply have gunned them in the back, or he could call out to them to give up their guns. Since he didn't fancy himself much of a back-shooter, he opted for the latter.

Standing up he called out, "Okay, boys, the game is over. Drop your guns."

Their reaction was immediate. They both turned and fired at him. Decker was a split second ahead of them and fired first.

His bullet struck one man and spun him around, although Decker couldn't see how badly he was hit. That man's shot went wild, but the other man's barely missed Decker and slapped into the side of the house.

Decker fired again, catching the second man solidly in the body. He yelled out, dropped his gun and slumped to the ground, his arms wrapped around himself.

The first man was still holding his gun and made an attempt to raise it into firing position.

"Don't try it, friend!" Decker shouted, aiming his gun at the man.

The man looked at Decker, figured his chances and then dropped the gun. From the looks of him he had been hit in the shoulder.

That was two, so where was the third man?

"Where's the other one?"

"What other one?" the man asked.

"The third man. Where is he?"

"Asleep."

"I don't buy—" Decker started to say and then he heard a board creak behind him. The third man was behind him and probably had no qualms about shooting him in the back. Could he turn and fire fast enough—and if he did, wouldn't the wounded man grab for his gun? One of them would get him.

"Decker!" someone shouted, and although it was a familiar voice, he didn't expect to hear it here.

He turned and the third man was aiming at him, about to fire. There was a shot, and the third man staggered to his left and fell—or was thrown—through the window into the house.

Decker turned back quickly and saw the wounded man reach his gun and close his hand over it. He fired, and the man cried out and fell over.

Now he rushed to the broken window to see how the third man was, but there was nothing to fear from him. He was lying in a pool of blood, some of it from cuts he'd suffered from the broken glass, but most of it from the bullet hole in the side of his neck.

Someone mounted the steps behind Decker and he turned, his gun ready, but relaxed when he saw the face of Tomàs de la Vega.

"Tomàs! What are you doing here?"

His friend smiled, holstered his gun and punched him in the nose.

"I owed you that!"

Epilogue

Moran and Crystal were both brought to the town doctor, and then laid up in a hotel room each. Decker arranged with the mayor and the town council to have each of them guarded. In Crystal's case it was unwarranted. She died barely an hour later.

Later, in the mayor's office, the mayor said, "Señor, we are in your debt for ridding us of these two . . . undesirables."

"I'm sure, Mr. Mayor, that if you and your town had been benefiting from their whorehouse they would have been much less undesirable."

The mayor cleared his throat and found that he had other work to do.

Later Decker and Anne had dinner in a café near the hotel. Tomàs had taken a hotel room and had turned in for the night. He and Decker would talk about the punch in the nose in the morning. In truth, Decker felt it was worth the punch to see his friend back on his feet again.

"Does it hurt?' Anne asked.

"What?"

"Your nose. It looks very red." She leaned over and touched it, and he winced.

"It's all right. Tomàs throws a pretty good punch. It's a good thing he's lost weight lately, though. He didn't have all that much to put behind it."

"Why did he hit you?"

"That's a long story. I'd rather not talk about that now. Instead, let's talk about what we are going to do," he said.

"About what?" she asked innocently.

She was dressed much more discreetly than she had been that first night he'd seen her at the Palace, this time in a simple blue dress, but she was no less lovely.

"About Moran."

"What about him?"

"Stop playing games, Anne. Crystal's yours, you came all this way to get her."

"You came all this way to get Moran."

"That's true, but you got him first."

"That's true, but then he got me and would have killed me if it wasn't for you."

"That's true."

"So what do we do about it?"

"That's what I was asking you."

"Well, I suppose we could split his reward," she said, stirring her coffee. "Then we'd both at least get something for the hardships we went through."

"What hardships? I tracked that man all the way from Colorado."

"And I tracked her all the way from Texas.

Besides, he almost killed me. You don't think that's a hardship?"

"Well, sure—"

"You don't think I should get something for being scared almost to death?"

"Well, yeah, but—"

"And besides, he would have shot you dead when you came through that door if it wasn't for me."

"Well . . . yeah . . ." Decker said, grudgingly.

She put her hand out and said, "Partners, then?"

He frowned, but finally figured that half a pie was better than none.

"All right, partners."

They shook hands but when he went to withdraw his she held on to it.

"How about we go up to your room and seal the bargain?" she asked, frankly.

He was surprised, and stammered.

"Uh, well, I, uh—"

"Decker," she said, surprised herself, "you're embarrassed."

He felt his face flush.

"Well, Anne, to tell you the truth, I'm not all that much of a ladies' man—"

"Well," she said, standing and pulling him to his feet, "for tonight, anyway, you're this lady's man."

Outlaws
PAUL BAGDON

Spur Award Finalist and Author of
Deserter and *Bronc Man*

Pound Taylor has just escaped from jail—and the hangman's noose—and he's eager to get back on the outlaw trail. For his gang he chooses his former cellmate and the father and brothers of his old partner, Zeb Stone. Pound wants to do things right, with lots of planning and minimum gunplay, but the Stone boys figure they can shoot first and worry about the repercussions later. Sure enough, that's just what they do—and they kill a man in the process. With the law breathing down their necks and the whole gang at one another's throats, Pound can see that hangman's noose getting closer all the time. Unless his friends kill him first!

ISBN 13: 978-0-8439-6073-0

The Classic Film Collection

The Searchers by Alan LeMay

Hailed as one of the greatest American films, *The Searchers*, directed by John Ford and starring John Wayne, has had a direct influence on the works of Martin Scorsese, Steven Spielberg, and many others. Its gorgeous cinematic scope and deeply nuanced characters have proven timeless. And now available for the first time in decades is the powerful novel that inspired this iconic movie. (Coming February 2009!)

Destry Rides Again by Max Brand

Made in 1939, the Golden Year of Hollywood, *Destry Rides Again* helped launch Jimmy Stewart's career and made Marlene Dietrich an American icon. Now available for the first time in decades is the novel that inspired this much-loved movie. (Coming March 2009!)

The Man from Laramie by T. T. Flynn

In its original publication, *The Man from Laramie* had more than half a million copies in print. Shortly thereafter, it became one of the most recognized of the Anthony Mann/Jimmy Stewart collaborations, known for darker films with morally complex characters. Now the novel upon which this classic movie was based is once again available—for the first time in more than fifty years. (Coming April 2009!)

The Unforgiven by Alan LeMay

In this epic American novel, which served as the basis for the classic film directed by John Huston and starring Burt Lancaster and Audrey Hepburn, a family is torn apart when an old enemy starts a vicious rumor that sets the range aflame. Don't miss the powerful novel that inspired the film the *Motion Picture Herald* calls "an absorbing and compelling drama of epic proportions." (Coming May 2009!)

To order a book or to request a catalog call:
1-800-481-9191
Books are also available at your local bookstore, or you can check out our Web site **www.dorchesterpub.com**.